The Cocooning

The Cocooning

A NOVEL BY

Sue Ann Kautz

WORD BOOKS
PUBLISHER
WACO, TEXAS

A DIVISION OF
WORD, INCORPORATED

THE COCOONING
A Novel by Sue Ann Kautz

Library of Congress Cataloging in Publication Data:

Kautz, Sue Ann, 1950–
    The cocooning.

    Summary: By hearing about an old fieldhand's experience with an angel, three adolescents find something to believe in beyond a materialistic world.
    [1. Christian life—Fiction] I. Title.
PS3561.A8678C6   1985   813'.54 [Fic]   85-3696
ISBN 0-8499-0492-7
ISBN 0-8499-3033-2 (pbk).

Printed in the United States of America

567898   FG   987654321

To my mother and father,
who have always believed

*Special acknowledgment to Howard McMillen,
a teacher and a gentle man.
Also to my Indiana State University thesis committee.*

The Cocooning

CHAPTER 1

THE WORST OF WINTER was over. The ground was still too cold to nurture plants or sprout seeds, and there were fires once again burning in six potbellied stoves in the little greenhouse on father's truck garden. While the temperature outside remained cool and unyielding, inside the greenhouse the atmosphere was like spring. Many of the seeds for the spring and summer were sown there.

Mr. Pearl returned to work nightly, firing the stoves and dozing in his rickety rocking chair with the sagging seat. The winter evenings were long, and I visited him often. We listened to the fire eating the coal, and we talked of possibilities. Mr. Pearl's hearth eyes kept me comfortable when the world was still full of icicles. The cold uncertainties that lingered after the fear of frost had passed crawled out the cracks and disappeared with his nearness.

When Mr. Pearl wasn't firing stoves or working in Father's fields, he lived in a cabin a few miles from our garden. He said that the land was a part of him, that he had known my grandfather and as a boy had worked on my great-grandfather's land. But I could not imagine Mr. Pearl's ever having worn the face of a child. It was my theory that one morning the earth had opened and out of its womb had stepped Mr. Pearl, new to the earth but already old. If man was made from clay, he was positive proof of it. The summer suns of nearly a century had cooked his skin until no one could recall when it had ever been flesh-colored and soft. It seemed as if it had always been a deep, baked brown covered with cracks and crevices. From early spring to late autumn Mr. Pearl worked from sunup to sundown. He often said he felt most alive when the sun shone and that it bothered him in autumn when the days grew shorter, as if he were losing precious time. I wondered if he had discovered a secret to immortality, or if, year after year, the sun had drunk up his mortal rights until he had become an earthen mummy, a treasure that scientists search for but rarely find.

Even the birds found Mr. Pearl enchanting. When Mr. Pearl whistled, the birds gathered by the dozens and perched on the electrical lines. Side by side they sat, as close as clothespins on a clothesline, befuddled that something so human could outdo their own melodious songs. But Mr. Pearl was like no other human being I had ever known. He was not educated in worldly ways. He could neither read nor write the alphabet, but he could read the signs of the sky, the earth, and the seasons as easily as most men read pages from a book. It was no wonder to me that he had seen an angel.

According to Mr. Pearl, the angel had visited him while I was still a baby in my mother's arms, and, like a Bible story, his experience had been repeated to me through the years. I loved to hear the tale; it somehow made my heart strong. Of all the talks and daydreaming hours Mr. Pearl and I spent together, his experience with the angel stayed afloat above them all like some unsinkable fishing cork in a stream of passing thoughts and words—never far from my sight, always bordering the visions of my mind.

Night seemed to unravel the mysteries of our souls and revive our yearnings to such restlessness that we often left the greenhouse and walked. We listened for the sounds of spring thaw that made frost into soft dew. We traveled over the familiar territories of memory and yarn as we walked through the woods and wished on stars. And we discussed the angel. It was necessary for Mr. Pearl to relive the experience, to pay tribute to the appearance of the angel. It made him tearful and it made me shiver and feel humble.

Spring was close and I was a year older than all the other

springs put together, or so it seemed. I was nearly thirteen. Mr. Pearl never changed; somehow the spinning earth had left its mark on him and gone its own way. But it was keeping time with me—tugging one way and pulling another until I was not sure who I was or where I belonged. I only knew that I was becoming less and less of a child and that I needed to cling to Mr. Pearl and his teachings.

One April night, we walked through the woods with a quiet respect. Something beautiful and deep rested beneath our feet: all the colors and creatures that would soon be waking. A sweet mist rose from little pockets of the earth and disappeared around my knees. There was a thin slice of moon and enough stars to cast a silver spell on the budding trees.

A train whistle whined in the distance. Those lonely whistles had wormed their way in and out of our daylight hours and deepest sleep for so many years that their echoes of steel and grinding wheels had become part of the harmony and quiet. And like the harmony and quiet, without explanation or end, were the talks between Mr. Pearl and me. We talked about everything in heaven, on earth, and in between—not foolish talk but serious thoughts.

"Now, Ada, as you know, God made man a little lower than the angels, but he loves man and angels equal." The stars had aroused a twinkling in Mr. Pearl's eyes and his whole earthy face shone.

"But men aren't as good as angels," I said, regarding my own sensibility on the subject. I was at the magic age of accountability to the Almighty, according to Mr. Pearl, and I was well-versed on the status of angels.

"Don't matter that men aren't as good. He loves men just the same. And a man can never be an angel, but an angel can be a man."

"How can an angel be a man?"

"An angel can disguise itself to look human. It says so in the Good Book—that you never know when you might be entertainin' an angel unaware."

"Oh. Of course. Now I remember. An angel can be like a man for a little while and then disappear." The wind stirred the stillness and I moved closer to him.

"Yes, Ada. That's what I mean." There was a satisfied gleam in his eyes.

"It's like a guardian angel, isn't it?"

"Good, Ada. In the time of need an angel can come near, but an angel can't always be seen the way the angel was seen by me."

"But Mr. Pearl, ever since you first told me about the angel, I have prayed mightily that I might see an angel too, but I've not seen a living sign. And I want to see an angel. I want to see one soon."

"Ada, just because you ain't seen an angel don't mean that someday you won't. If you believe you will, then you will. Do you believe?"

"Some days I do and some days I don't. I guess if God hears me on the right day, I will. But if he hears me on the wrong day, I won't. Maybe it's better that I don't for the sake of my asthma. Lord knows it would most likely scare the breath right out of me."

"Now Ada, I told you not to talk about the angel in that tone of voice. The angel wasn't something to get shaky over. It was something to speak about in a whisper, like in a prayer."

"I understand, Mr. Pearl, but I would still be scared."

"Most grown men would be scared if they saw an angel, no matter how brave they was," Mr. Pearl said. "Or they wouldn't believe what they was seein'." He paused a moment to look up at the audience of stars. "But nobody believes in angels anymore."

His voice sounded sad but then revived when he declared, "But what I seen, I seen, and nobody can take that away from me. They can call me a liar a hundred times, but they can't change the truth."

"It's peculiar how some people won't believe the truth," I said. "They'd sooner believe a lie. I believe in angels without a doubt!" I wanted to reestablish our bond of belief. "Someday they'll all know it was so."

"Don't matter." He put his arm around my shoulder, the sleeve of his denim jacket brushing my cheek and smelling of coal dust and smoke, a winter fragrance he often wore.

"Well, who are 'they' anyway?" I felt my rage rise to cursing proportions, but I held my tongue. "They're just a bunch of heathens in the night."

I had made the mistake of telling a few people about Mr. Pearl and the angel when I was too young to understand the consequences. My first-grade teacher had sent a note home suggesting that Mr. Pearl was a bad influence on my overpowered imagination. Some people had even accused Mr. Pearl of being senile, but my mother and father had defended him and told me, "Ada, never you mind!"

From then on, Mr. Pearl and I had protected the story the way people protect something fragile and sacred. When farmers stopped to complain to Father about the dry spells and the cucumber beetles, Mr. Pearl joined in and discussed the problems with them. We had never again talked to outsiders about the supernatural—only about what could be seen with the naked eye and touched with human hands.

That night, after we had reveled over the angel and talked about invisible things, and after Mr. Pearl had gone his way to the greenhouse to tend to the stoves and I had gone my way back to the house and into my bedroom, I tried to sleep. But I could think only of angels. I stared at the shelf that held angel statues of every shape, size, and color—angels that I had collected in the twelve years Mr. Pearl and I had been together. One angel stood out among the rest, the angel Mr. Pearl had carved for me out of wood from a pin-oak branch.

Sitting on my window sill was an angel windchime that waited for the spring wind to spin it into heavenly music—a music that only such a willing spirit could understand.

I did not want to lose what beliefs I had in order to grow, although I was not quite sure what my beliefs were. I was a pitcher full of fantasies, perhaps, but still a pitcher full. Whether water or light, did the pitcher have to spill in order for a child to grow? I did not know where the child would go when the woman came.

Would I think differently? Would I regret Mr. Pearl and all those dream seeds he had planted in me? I, who had grown up listening to stories of angels instead of folklore and fairy tales, knew of no other way.

CHAPTER 2

"Your grandma believed in angels," Father said. We were discussing angels a few weeks later at breakfast.

"Did she ever see one?" I blindly buttered my bread.

"No. But she fed every hobo that came begging at her door. Bread and butter and coffee too." Father sported his story with long pauses while he chewed and swallowed his bacon. "She must have fed a hundred hobos one year when times were bad."

"That's because Grandma thought she might be entertaining an angel unaware!" I said. "There's talk about it in the Bible."

"That's true," Father nodded. "Your grandma was scared she'd turn one away."

"You've been talking to our authority on the subject, haven't you?" Mother smiled at me, not mocking my delight.

"Maybe we should start feeding hobos too." I had been told that hobos carried all their belongings on their backs, ate from tin cans, cursed like hardened criminals, and fought like pirates. Although not considered supernatural, they would have been an exciting substitute.

"No, Ada. That's unthinkable." Father saw Mother's sleepy eyes widen. "Hobos are a lazy bunch without a working will or muscle."

"I thought you liked angels."

"I do. But we're talking about hobos now."

"Well, don't you think it's wonderful that Mr. Pearl saw an angel right in our very own field?"

17

"Sure I do. The more heaven we have on this earth, the better." Father finished his eggs with the usual satisfaction. There was thunder in the distance. "Sounds like all hell's going to break loose out there any minute."

"But it's Saturday and the sun's out." I had not looked at the weather conditions, but I could feel the sun extending its reach through the kitchen window to the back of my head. My scalp felt as warm as my bare feet that nestled deep into Tippy Ten's fur. I had a habit of hiding my dog under the table, as breakfast was my most dreaded meal.

"More eggs, Ada?" Mother asked. "My you're a hungry little animal."

"I guess." I hated eggs, but I knew Tippy Ten would devour them. He gently nibbled my toes when he was ready for another portion of my plate's holdings. This routine was usually successful enough to eliminate my plate of eggs, with Mother none the wiser, but that morning I exhausted four fists full of scrambled eggs, still unable to keep Tippy's appetite under control. I could hear his jaws snap and feel his saliva on my feet. His tail thumped impatiently on the linoleum. I slipped him my grapefruit-half in quiet desperation. When Mother saw it missing from my plate, she questioned me.

"Ada, did you give Daddy your grapefruit?"

"No . . . uh . . . I—"

Tippy thumped his tail again, this time audible to Mother's senses.

"Tippy Ten!" She bent down in time to touch noses with him. "There'll be a pound of dirt on the floor from his fur. Come on, Tippy! Outside, boy!" She opened the door and pointed her slender finger in the appropriate direction. Tippy Ten left the kitchen reluctantly with the taste of my breakfast still on his lips.

"Did you eat after him?" Mother stared at my greasy hands the way an aristocrat would gaze at a peasant's pleasure. "You'll catch worms from him, not to mention germs. Go wash."

"Tippy Ten is not just another animal. Mother, you know you love him." The word *love* usually transformed mother's fury to forgiveness in an instant.

"Of course I love him, but you'd set a plate for him at the table if I allowed it."

"The dog's smart enough to use a fork and spoon." Father had a schoolboy's attachment for Tippy Ten. He had rescued Tippy from death row at the dog pound for the price of two dollars. The dog was supposedly ferocious, but Father's keen sense of kindness had overruled the opinions of the men who tried to talk him out of taking Tippy Ten. I had been a year old when Father brought Tippy Ten home, and the dog and I had been constant companions ever since. The idea of Tippy Ten eating from the table wasn't unfeasible.

Father laughed until he stood up and slipped on the grapefruit-half that Tippy had rejected. The rind stuck to the heel of his shoe, and he had to catch himself awkwardly in time to prevent a fall. Then he grabbed his jacket and grumbled something about the storm as he closed the kitchen door behind him.

"The sky's turning as black as a man's hat." Mother stared out of the window watching Father walk toward the field. She rested her chin in her hands and leaned against the cabinet. She had the most delicate lines and movement; I had never seen an awkward stroke betray her. Considering Mother's beauty and Father's kind temperament, I was certain I was an orphan that someone had abandoned on their doorstep.

THE STORM APPROACHED from the west, the fiercest direction for an April storm to be born. Mr. Pearl and I watched the massive cloud formation's threatening face. Was this to be spring? Spring looked to be an angry creature with a mean jaw. Like a giant's imposing shadow the thunderheads loomed, smothering the sunlight and draining the landscape of its colors. Spring without and within—I was akin to it because I was unable to control the weather of my own body and soul.

There were days when a heaviness swelled in my chest, producing pain that stifled every breath until my breathing became a tiresome routine that other people experienced only when they ran too far, too fast without stopping.

"Now, Ada, "Mr. Pearl preached, "the reason for your asthma is that you're fightin' everything. A body ain't able to take so many wars ragin' inside it without them wars leavin' their mark. Your mark happens to be your bad breathin'."

"That's ridiculous!" I raved at him, but my breathing had become increasingly worse that year until I was forced to wear an asthma mask. I was allergic to weed pollen and dust, and this made me useless to Father.

"I'm positive he wished he had a son," I said.

"Naaaaaah." Mr. Pearl's mouth and jaw crumpled up like a shriveled apple. "All sons ain't the same. Some boys hate to work in the dirt same as some girls. People think they're too good for the dirt but the dirt gets 'em all in the end." The sky was growing darker and it looked as if the world would end within the hour.

"Think there'll be a tornado?" I asked. Mr. Pearl was attempting to finish sowing seeds in the east field, picking them up in tender pinches from his palm and sprinkling them.

"Don't think so. Those clouds are angry, but they ain't low. The bad clouds are low. They almost touch the ground. That's when you worry."

"Well, I'd give my eyeteeth to see a tornado." I stared into the clouds and watched for whirling motions. Mr. Pearl continued to sow, his hands moving with perfect accuracy.

"A tornado moved down Springhill Road and up the hill by the cemetery about fifty years ago. Killed a lot of people," he said.

"Was it a big one?"

"Big as I ever want to see. Sounded like a freight train. The sky turned green." He looked up at me long enough to drop a seed packet into my hand. "If you never see a twister, you can call yourself lucky. Now don't just stand there gawking at the sky. Help me finish and be gentle with your sowing. Treat these seeds like little babies."

"I guess I'll never see a funnel cloud or nothing. I'd be satisfied with an angel. Mr. Pearl, do you think that the angel was bringing a message to you?"

"I think so." He smoothed and patted the dirt over the seeds. His hands looked ancient, like they had been buried for a century.

"Then tell me," I insisted, "what did the visit of the angel mean?"

"It's the kind of thing you can't put into words," he answered in a murmur.

"Then it's a secret, and you said you'd never keep a secret from me." It wasn't what he said, but what he didn't say that kept the truth hidden. Like being allowed in all the rooms of a grand old house while one room remained forbidden. "I'm going to Old Woman Wenzel. She'll tell me. She reads tea leaves and can tell your past, present, and future just by looking at you."

"Those fortune tellers just mess with spirits of the dead," he said. "They don't know nothing about what God's planned. They play the devil's games."

There were stories that the dishes on Old Lady Wenzel's shelves shook and the drawers in her cabinets opened and closed without the help of human hands. But people visited her daily to have their fortunes told, and none of them had come up missing yet.

"Maybe so, but Rexy went and Old Lady Wenzel told her she'd find money and break a bone. The very same week Rexy found money in a jar and she broke her toe."

Mr. Pearl spit on the ground in protest.

"And she removes warts for a nickel apiece. You show her the wart and pay her, and they disappear overnight."

"Who'd that ever happen to?"

"Clarence Huff. I heard him talking about it one day during school. He raised his pants legs and showed everyone in the class where the warts had been."

"Did you ever see the warts before?"

"No. But you couldn't have paid me to look at Clarence Huff's legs for any other reason before that. Clarence said she sits across from folks in a chair and this king-sized Siamese cat sits on her lap. Before she talks she closes her eyes and rubs her hands together fast and hard, like this." I did my best to demonstrate. Just talking about her gave me goose bumps. I watched a population of them spread across my arms, producing a tingle up my spine.

"Ada, you're making a serious mistake if you go to see her."

"Why?"

"I done told you."

"Give me another reason," I persisted.

"She gives you nightmares," he said triumphantly.

Old Lady Wenzel had come to Father's one summer to buy vegetables, and when she smiled at me her two gold front teeth had reflected the sunlight. That same night I had dreamed of her standing by my bedroom door with those same two teeth sending out a ray of light.

"You're right," I said. "She's as scary as Halloween."

"Here comes the wind," Mr. Pearl said, slowly getting to his feet. The wind grew so gusty that our clothing flapped. A few maple branches cracked and snapped free. The birds in their flight for safety battled the currents. "Get out of this dust before your asthma takes you." Mr. Pearl led me away from the field and toward the greenhouse. Then the rain began to fall in thick splatterings. It was a cold rain that we took shelter from. Once inside the greenhouse shed I sat in Mr. Pearl's rocking chair and my throat thickened.

"Now you done it, Ada." Mr. Pearl tried to make me comfortable by adjusting the back cushion.

"I didn't do a thing. That's what's so sickening about it." There was a pain growing in my rib cage.

"Where's that darn contraption the doctor gave you? You should have been wearing it," Mr. Pearl said. My asthma mask was a gaudy device that covered my nose and mouth like a square bird's beak. It kept itself in place by an elastic strap that stretched around the back of my head.

"I hate it!" I pulled out the mask which had lately become a tenant of my right pocket unless necessity called it to action.

Mr. Pearl knew when not to be sympathetic. He looked at the mask as if it were a thing of beauty. "Ada, complaining never makes a sick man well. It just makes him sicker."

"I'm sick all right." The sound of my breathing was as irritating as grinding gears that needed to be greased. The doctor called it "wheezing." I put the mask on reluctantly.

"You ain't as sick as you think" Mr. Pearl said. "Growin' pains is all that's wrong with you. Even your breathing will calm. These seeds probably feel the same way before they sprout into more important things. Look over there." He pointed to a space where the seeds had poked their little green heads through the cracks in the sand. "Change comes about with the work of our own heart and hands. Even a seed has to push itself up from the ground."

"I do feel buried alive, if that's a growing sign." I had removed my mask to speak; otherwise my voice sounded low and muffled like I was talking in a tunnel.

"I ain't worried about you a bit." Mr. Pearl tapped the toe of his workshoe on the cement, then anxiously scraped his soles on the coal grit. "Ada, you got more than your share of common sense and some uncommon sense besides. That's why you best stay away from Old Lady Wenzel and let the Lord provide."

"I just don't know." I rested my head against the back of the chair and listened to the gloom.

THE WIND DROVE THE RAIN into the barn's wood grain, darkening the color of the worn red paint. The storm left a shine upon the greenhouse glass. In the countryside, the leaves and blades of grass and every crevice in the bark of the trees were cleansed. There was a deeper vein of green in everything.

When my wheezing subsided, I was out roaming the fields again, hot on the trail of adventure. It was then that I saw a flock of pigeons land on a strip of freshly plowed ground. City pigeons often flew to the country when food was scarce, and there must have been fifty of them, mostly gray, but also a few white ones adding dimension to the flock. A nervous species perhaps, or maybe they were just cautious in strange surroundings. They flew at once and landed together in different spots on the field. One pigeon lagged behind. It struggled to fly, but faltered. My parents had always said, "You can't catch a wild thing, child." I rushed to the barn repeating, "I can. I can. I can."

I took some heavy twine, tied a lasso knot, and headed for the far end of the field. I unwound my twine and waited for the injured pigeon to step into my primitive trap. It seemed like I had waited for an hour when finally the pigeon stepped its foot into the loop and I quickly pulled the string around it. The pigeon twitched, nodded, and tripped without getting away. It had an agreeable gait, despite its limp wing that dragged. It kept a steady pace, bobbing its head to the strut of its feet as I led it to the barn on its twine leash. It was a glorious moment for me. The pigeon's need gave me some merciful power to hover over it and call it mine.

Mr. Pearl was stacking baskets and whistling a duet with the wind that still whined through the cracks in the barn boards when I walked in. Tippy Ten napped at Mr. Pearl's feet. When the pigeon followed after me, Tippy merely raised his head and sniffed in the bird's direction, but Mr. Pearl took one look and his lip quivered down to his chin.

"It's wet and its wing won't work," I said. The pigeon's wing hung unfolded like a feather fan. "I known what you think of pigeons, but . . . I'll train it. It's friendly and . . ."

The more seriously I defended the pigeon, the harder Mr. Pearl tried not to react; this caused his tear ducts to swell and then burst with sunny relief. I was totally enraged with him.

"You're shameful! Stop laughing at it! I'm calling this pigeon 'Puddin.' Poor Puddin, probably in pain," I said, stroking the pigeon's back. "I'll make it better."

"You're goin' to fix this pigeon so it'll fly and eat your daddy's grain?" He was laughing unashamedly by then.

"It's going to be a pet. Weren't you listening? How would you like to be replaced by a pigeon, old man?"

"Pigeons make good pets," Mr. Pearl nodded. "But pigeon lice might get you. Ain't you heard about bird lice?"

Immediately my skin itched, but I was determined not to scratch for the mere principle that this pigeon did not possess all the foul qualities Mr. Pearl presupposed.

"I'm not afraid to tend to the sick for fear of disease," I said importantly. "This pigeon is not dirty. It's clean. It may be homely, but it's not dirty!"

Mr. Pearl wept with laughter. Then he bent down and smoothed the pigeon's feathers with one thick finger. "He's been roughed up by the storm," he said. And with the serious face of a surgeon, he examined the injured wing while the bird lay in my cupped hands. The bird did not resist our attention, but its heart beat like a rapid little drum through its ruffled feathers.

"He won't die, will he?" I could not see how its small heart could continue to beat at such a fast pace.

"Pigeons don't die from broken wings," Mr. Pearl said. He went to the seed cupboard and found tape and twine scissors. He was gentle and quick about mending the injury. The pigeon perked up its head as Mr. Pearl whistled to calm it. After a few tedious minutes, he took a deep breath and said, "That ought to do it." The pigeon held its wing lopsidedly, but I knew the healing would begin.

"Now, where you goin' to put it?" Mr. Pearl searched the barn, inspecting bushel baskets and lettuce containers.

"I know just the place!" I handed him the pigeon's leash and ran to the back of the barn.

"Ada, you ain't supposed to go up to the loft! It's against your daddy's wishes. It ain't safe. I'll go."

"If it's not safe for me, then it's not safe for you." I hurried more.

"Ada, come back here. One of the boards might be rotten and you'd fall through, break an arm or leg or anything."

"You can't tell me what to do!" I said with sweet rebellion. I had never climbed the rickety ladder to the barn loft alone. The few times I had been allowed to climb, Father had accompanied me with warnings of wasp nests and hives of bees. The ladder was steep and led straight up into a dark balcony filled with baskets and containers with the usual amount of stale hay and straw—a disaster area for asthma victims. It was only a moment before my feet pressed cranky boards. I moved with caution, allowing time for my eyes to adjust to the splinters of menacing darkness.

"Ada!" Mr. Pearl stood nervously beneath the loft and looked up through the floor boards. I stood over him and made sinister noises. Bits of hay seeped through the cracks and fell upon his hat and shoulders. He was still holding the twine connected to the pigeon's leg. "Ada, I ain't watchin' this darn pigeon another minute. Get a melon crate and come back here."

The loft suffered from neglect. I moved cautiously, knowing that at any moment Mr. Pearl might witness a leg or two dangling through a space where a floor board failed to give support. I chose the closest crate for safety's sake.

"Get down here and attend to this pigeon! You'll be sick up there. Don't say you ain't been warned. Your daddy is goin' to give me heck for lettin' you do this."

"Don't get yourself in an uproar," I growled, tossing the melon crate over the edge. I made my descent sneezing, which gave Mr. Pearl even more cause to complain. We rarely disagreed, but there were uncertainties growing between us, too close to betrayal or mistrust to be openly discussed.

"Child, you do like to disobey," he grumbled helplessly.

We found a dry spot in which to place the melon crate, soon to become an airy abode for my pigeon. I immediately set up housekeeping by filling two jar lids with water and grain. When Puddin was finally placed inside, he inspected his domain and responded by contentedly clucking deep in his throat.

"He likes it!" I was exuberant. "I want Puddin to be a homing pigeon. Someday he won't have to be caged and when his wing heals, he can fly, but he won't fly away."

"Dream on, Ada." Mr. Pearl studied the bird as it stepped into its water dish, upsetting it. "Don't act smart enough to me."

"I'll call him and he'll fly to me. You'll see."

"Maybe." Mr. Pearl took a deep breath, exhaling burdensome regret. "But Ada, I been thinking. It's a shame you don't have anyone to call your friend 'cept for an old man, an old dog, and a lame pigeon." He massaged his eyes before he bothered to look up at me. Maybe he could see the future clearer by rubbing away that familiar closeness. Whether near-sighted or far-sighted, he saw me from new directions where I had yet to be. "I don't mean there's anything pitiful about birds or animals or me being old, except that you're young and should be getting out and meeting the new. Someday you're going to outgrow me, and I want you to. It's only natural."

Mr. Pearl's words severed the excitement of the day. My eyes searched the barn floor for a cool recovery. I looked up at him and gave him a little push with my hand, more from fear than anger. "How can you say that? There's no one in the world as good as you. Not even a high and mighty angel can hold a candle to you!"

He was irreplaceable. I had spent many hours wading in creek bottoms looking for lost treasures, only to find Mr. Pearl's eyes reflecting into mine.

"I mean it, sister." His eyes were sparkling now, but still he badgered me. "You need to get out and make friends with people your own age. Nice, ordinary friends."

"And just what do you mean by 'ordinary'?" It was he who had taught me to see the unusual as common until I had lost sight of what others might call normal relationships.

"Kids your own age at school."

"I hate Mount Mercer. It's a school for misfits. They're all as strange as Freddie Moulton. Well, almost."

"Freddie Moulton likes you," Mr. Pearl chuckled. "He told me so."

"I hate Freddie Moulton! I hate him and I happen to know our hatred is mutual! Have you betrayed me? Have you told him anything different? I'll never forgive you if you have. I'll disown you. I'll . . ."

"Nope. I didn't say a word 'cept I like you too."

CHAPTER 3

I AM NOT SORRY that Freddie Moulton shared in the things that were to come. His transformation was a part of my own. Until that spring Freddie had been an example of the unchanging. He was the same fat intolerable brat that I had known since the first grade. Not only was Freddie thirty pounds overweight, but he also had pendulum eyes that moved from side to side without ever resting. The doctors said that even when Freddie slept his eyes were moving, and that daylight appeared to be dusk from Freddie's point of view.

Mount Mercer was a private school for students like Freddie who could not adjust to normal learning situations. There were stutterers, deaf children, three boys in wheel chairs, and students with personality problems too complex to discuss with anyone other than a psychiatrist. So when Mother expressed to Mrs. Moulton, who lived on our rural route, my acute embarrassment over wearing my asthma mask, which solicited stares, sneers, and giggles from fellow students, Mrs. Moulton suggested that I try Mount Mercer Private School. Mount Mercer was air-conditioned and my asthma mask would not have to be worn there.

My parents arranged for Mrs. Moulton to drive me to and from Mount Mercer, an uncomfortable situation for me. I soon developed a natural slump from sitting low in the seat so as not to be noticed in the same car with Freddie. Not that there was anyone at Mount Mercer I cared to impress! Out of a seventh-grade class of ten students I did not cultivate one close friend.

The following Monday morning was no exception to my daily agony. When the sun crept over the high windows of the schoolroom, I thought of how the very same sun was transforming the fields of dew and making the morning glories bloom.

"Ada! Ada! Pssst." School with Freddie was an extension of my misery. I ignored him. I pictured Father and Mr. Pearl walking out and handling the plants again and again. I could almost hear Mr. Pearl whistling as he pushed the hand plow while Tippy followed after him.

"Ada! Psssssssst." I pretended he did not exist. I could hear the doves cooing drowsy songs in the pine and I felt my energy slipping away exactly as I did on those warm butter days when Mr. Pearl and I rested beneath the pin-oak shade and told stories.

"Ada Kross. Pssssssssssst!" I daydreamed whenever possible, content to be alone without a thought to share with anyone.

"Ada Kristina Kross. Psssssst. Psssssst." My daydreams were endless. Because of them, I survived. Even when Freddie demanded my attention, which happened at the most inappropriate times.

"Psssssssst. Ada. Psssssssst."

"Freddie Moulton!" Mrs. Oliver pounded her fist upon her desk. "Come here at once and bring me what you have in your hands!" Freddie got out of his seat and approached Mrs. Oliver in a slow waddle.

"Is this the way a thirteen-year-old should act?" Mrs. Oliver held up the beheaded flower stems in her hand. Freddie had been entertaining the class by popping dandelion heads into his mouth and eating them. Mrs. Oliver was very upset. Her mouth puckered and her eyes twitched like a cat's.

"Freddie, I've warned you about showing off like this. You've disrupted my class once too often."

Freddie turned his back to Mrs. Oliver and smiled at the class, who returned his look with laughter. I was surprised to see that the class had a sense of humor.

"No laughing, class! No laughing!" Mrs. Oliver shouted. She turned Freddie around briskly with surprising strength. "Freddie, clean out your pockets," she demanded.

Freddie pulled a yo-yo, a candy bar, some black licorice sticks, a wad of string, and a war medal out of his pockets. The war medal had belonged to Freddie's father, who had died in a foreign war before Freddie was ever born. Freddie set the belongings on Mrs. Oliver's desk, almost too eagerly to be seriously repentent.

"Now take off your glasses." Mrs. Oliver pulled out a paddle as Freddie took off his glasses and leaned heavily against the desk with his hands. The paddle hit his backside with a smarting whack. Another whack followed. Freddie smiled, but his face ripened to the tune of the class's laughter. The class laughed even more, knowing that they shouldn't. Some struggled to keep their laughter inside of their hands.

When the dismissal bell rang, I ran from the scene, sick with a putrid disgust. Freddie found his glasses, stuffed his pockets with his possessions, and ran after me.

"Ada! Ada, wait!" He huffed and puffed, looking like a giant beach ball, his stomach bouncing beneath his red and white striped t-shirt.

"Freddie," I snarled vehemently, "If you don't stop acting like we're friends. . . . I don't want our names spoken in the same breath."

"You're nobody special, Ada Kross," he said. "You're nothing but a dirt farmer's daughter." He stuck out his bulging chest. "My father was a decorated war hero."

"If it weren't for dirt farmers, you wouldn't be so fat and sassy." I gave him a shove for the pure joy of it, and watched him tumble helplessly down six stairs, bounce off the wall, and fall backwards to the floor. He didn't feel a thing with his natural padding. When he managed to get back on his feet, he shook his fist at me and screamed.

"Just for that, I'm going to give you a big kiss!" He puckered up his hog lips and moved toward me.

"You do and I'll puke on you." I slapped his face promptly.

"Ada Kross, you can walk home for that. I'm telling my mother. You're nothing but a skinny little ugly runt! Skinny! Skinny! Skinny! Ugly! Ugly! Ugly! Runt! Runt! Runt!" He stumbled out the door before I could defend myself verbally or otherwise. And whatever he told his mother proved successful enough for her to leave me stranded at the school. I called Father, who sent Mr. Pearl to my rescue in his black, shiny pickup truck.

MR. PEARL AND I drove home on the back roads beside creek beds and fence rows. The truck rattled and made new holes in the road that dipped and curved and passed through covered bridges. There was the bittersweet scent of honeysuckle along the roadside and dogwood that painted the woods with a new white life. Gazing at it all made me feel plainer than ever, a mere human being saddled with a soul and brain, instead of the perfection of flowers, the gracefulness of running horses, the dramatic beauty of painted butterfly wings.

"You ain't plain. You're gettin' prettier every day," Mr. Pearl said. The bumps in the road were jarring his hat and jaw. Freddie was to blame for my already deflated ego. I worried that I was pigeon-toed and knock-kneed, that I was skinny and walked like an ostrich. There was a space between my two front teeth that my parents referred to as a "pleasant gap." My hair and eyes were mud-colored. Mother's hair was golden and her eyes were green.

"I'm plain, I tell you. I can see. I've got a mirror. And today Freddie Moulton called me a skinny, ugly runt three times. Not that I care what he thinks, because I hate him with all my heart. I hate him! I especially hate him because—" I wasn't about to discuss Freddie's attempt to steal a kiss. It was the worst embarrassment of my adolescent history. "Just believe me when I say I hate him."

Mr. Pearl looked at me like he didn't know what hating meant.

"Well, I do hate him," I said. "I told you that. What he thinks doesn't count. Tell me what you think. It seems that if I was pretty, I'd know without a shadow of a doubt, but since I'm not sure, I'm probably not pretty."

"You make plain sound like a dirty word," Mr. Pearl said.

"You're saying I'm plain, aren't you? Well, go ahead and say it."

He shook his head. "I ain't sayin' you're plain. Heaven forbid. But in my day a plain woman was considered the prettiest kind. You couldn't wash her beauty away. Sweet Cindy was plain and beautiful." Mr. Pearl's voice became sentimental. "A man couldn't have had a prettier wife. I miss her," he said in a whisper.

"I don't know why I asked you. You're one-sided. Everything is beautiful to you. Is Mother plain or beautiful?"

"Your mother is plain and beautiful like you'll be someday," he replied.

"I think Mother is plain and beautiful too, but you're saying I'm plain without the beautiful. Isn't that what you're saying?" I put my face next to his and tried to capture his complete attention.

"Ada, I don't have to look at you close as that. I know your face by heart and I tell you, you're pretty now. And someday, Ada, I'll be workin' in the field and I'll look up and see a young woman walkin' toward me. She'll be just like a vision, and I'll study her for a minute thinkin' she's a stranger, but you know who she'll be?"

"Who?" I asked, mostly out of duty.

"Ada, that young woman will be you." For the first time since we had left the school he took his eyes off the road and looked at me.

"I didn't say anything about wanting to become a woman," I said self-consciously. Beauty made a girl into a woman, notwithstanding that beauty came from within. But it was outer beauty that I was concerned about.

"Don't worry," he said. "You'll have plenty of time to get used to it."

It was Mother who made me worry about my inheritance. Mother's temperament was as sweet as country frosting. She was delicate and refined like Queen Anne's lace that grew wild in the summertime. Sometimes we were the best of friends; she seemed to be a child like me, only older, with an identity that would someday be mine.

Mother's beauty made me want to cry. She was happy and I suddenly was not and did not know why. She had always hurt when I hurt, and I knew she would have wept with me over the things that were hers so effortlessly, but I could not confide in her. Mother had arrived on the other side of the struggle, and this made her seem unapproachable. All of the cares of life were absent in her presence, and it was frightening to look at her and wonder if it was painful to grow so lovely.

CHAPTER 4

I WANTED TO REST—not under pin-oak trees or in peaceful night sleeps, but to rest again in happiness without want or need. For so long I had been a resting child, but when change began it could not be quenched; it remolded the old and uncovered the new. It was this pitcher that spilled and refilled until I remained true to Ada Kross in name only, until Mr. Pearl spoke to me as if a part of my person were already a memory.

I had not wished for change. Spring brought me always to the pin oaks that never changed. The pin oaks were impartial listeners, quiet friends. Their sloping branches formed a tent beneath which Mr. Pearl, Tippy Ten, and I had rested every spring and summer from the time the noon whistle blew until the one-o'clock freight train bolted past on the railroad track that ran parallel to our land. It was the pin oaks' solidarity that I clung to—and of course to Mr. Pearl, who like the pin oaks had grown thicker skin and collected time within.

We met under the pin oaks for the first time that spring, the trees towering over us and enclosing us with their familiarity. Before Mr. Pearl brushed away the dead leaves that had collected at the foot of the largest tree, he embraced the pin oak by wrapping his arms around the trunk of it, as if in doing so he was given added time and strength.

The ground we sat upon was not totally thawed, and it chilled the backs of our legs through our trousers. We sat very close, leaning our backs against the tree trunk, shoulders touching shoulders and heads touching. The leaves with their flat faces and new thin lives did not as yet hinder the remarkably yellow sun from pouring down and covering us with a thick warm light. The pin-oak leaves would later become dense and deep, and there would be green foliage to create privacy from the world and the heat. As the work became hotter in the fields, the pin oaks would become more protective. Soon the sun would no longer be allowed inside. But that day the air was pleasant and cool. The spring sun pushed the clouds aside and overflowed, pouring over us in a golden funnel until it seemed that we would both glow and that the purity of it would take us and make us immortal.

"Here it is spring again." I sniffed the newness and the old, too.

"Yep. And here's me and you," Mr. Pearl said.

He opened his metal lunch bucket and took out a peanut-butter sandwich. His face shone like tarnished copper. Tippy Ten wedged through the lower pin-oak branches that hugged the ground. He stared hungrily at Mr. Pearl's food.

"I don't suppose you would want to whistle, would you?" I asked him. His songs were so enticing and they reminded me of simpler times.

"Not while I'm eating peanut butter, but I will directly. Just give me a minute." He threw a piece of his sandwich to Tippy, who caught it with the grace of a crocodile.

"Ada, do you love these trees?" Mr. Pearl asked me. He stopped chewing his sandwich and listened intently for my answer. It was too quiet for comfort.

"Of course I do." I searched his gaze for some purpose, but his eyes were more gentle than kind.

"How much do you love these trees?"

"I love them as much as anyone can love a tree, I guess."

"Why do you love them?" he asked. If he were scolding me, there would not be such caution in his voice.

"I love them because they're big and old. Because they've always been here for you and me." The silence between us seemed threatening. "Nobody's going to cut them down, are they?"

"No. But Ada, someday you're goin' to grow up and move away from this land. Will you stop lovin' these trees then?"

I looked up into the lacework of leaves that enclosed us. "No. Never." An unexplainable sorrow overwhelmed me; a dread for the future made me sad. It was the first time I realized that, even though Mr. Pearl's world was mine, my world was going to be more.

"Mr. Pearl, have you ever been homesick?" I knew that was the feeling I was experiencing—like a premonition.

"Ada, I'm homesick now," he gently sighed.

"Homesick . . . how?"

"Homesick the way you feel homesick for the spring in the dead of winter. And I'm homesick for Sweet Cindy. But I know she's waitin' for me in the by and by."

"Sweet Cindy can wait forever as far as I'm concerned," I said. "Too many people here you've got to think about."

"I met your new neighbor today," Mr. Pearl said. He used his words to lead me astray. "The man who moved into the Bell Farm? He's a professor. Seems real mannerly. Says he wants to do a little gardening on the side. I'm glad somebody is going to put that Bell ground to good use again."

"I thought I heard the dinner bell ringing last night," I said. "You know, that dinner bell under the eaves of the big gray barn. It's been a long time since we heard any life over there. Do they have any children?"

"They have a girl." Mr. Pearl looked at me and grinned.

"What kind of daughter do they have?" I knew she had to be the perfect professor's child.

"Don't know," Mr. Pearl said. "But I saw her waiting for the school bus by her mailbox this morning. She looked about your size."

"Is she pretty or plain?"

"I didn't get a good look at her. You'll have to invite her over. Then you can feast your eyes full. She might make you a good friend."

"Good nothin'." I kicked up a little dirt with the toe of my shoe. "I probably won't have a thing in common with her. She's probably shy with an unbelievably high I.Q. Not down to earth like I am."

"Ada, I've never known you to be down to earth." Mr. Pearl gave me a curious glance. "You've always been dancing on some cloud."

"I know I won't like her. She's probably a cat person too."

"It's cats you're allergic to, not the people." Mr. Pearl sounded seriously concerned. "I'm almost ashamed of you when you talk like that. I'm telling you, Ada; you need a good friend."

"I need nothing of the kind." A quiet pain cornered me and slipped out with my fury. "Convenience for convenience's sake is not the way to choose a friend. I've got you, don't I?"

"Ada, it don't do no good to talk to you. Miss Hard Head needs nothin' of the kind."

"Mr. Pearl, I don't know what's wrong with you." My heart had been throbbing with the fears of Mr. Pearl's abandonment of me. "You're different, and I don't like it."

"I ain't different." He took off his mangled hat and adjusted its bent brim. He was deep in thought as he brushed off the dirt and planted it comfortably back on his head.

"Don't deny it. You're acting strange," I said.

"Ada, you're in a nasty mood." His smile should have been consoling. "Look up. The sun is breaking through the clouds and the sky is soooo blue. My blue heaven."

"Stop talking about the sky and heaven. It's always blue and it'll always be blue. Blue. Blue. Blue. But you're different."

Mr. Pearl reached in his pocket and pulled out an arrowhead. "I found me another arrowhead yesterday when I was hoeing the west field. I saved it for you." He held the arrowhead in his palm with all the intentions of giving it to me.

"Those Indians are dead and gone and I don't want another arrowhead. I tell you, you're different."

I knew every wrinkle in his face—where they folded and how they changed when he scowled, whistled, and smiled. I was familiar with the way his pants hung and certain places where the cuffs dragged the ground and where his shoes were leather worn and where, inside the creases, they had hardly lost their shine. Looking at Mr. Pearl made me feel lost somehow. I hated the thickening veils between us—the veils of time that could not be pushed aside. I knew that throwing my arms around Mr. Pearl and repeating "I love you" a thousand times would not change what must be. They would not stop the cocooning. I hid my hands in my face and cried.

"Shhhhhhh. Don't cry, Ada. Listen." Mr. Pearl tried to comfort me. "Listen. God is talking to the trees." I listened as the sun parted the branches and lit up the moss and dampness around our feet. "Now the leaves will soon be answering," he whispered again. And as he spoke, a gust of wind picked up his words, and every leaf became a part of a thousand shushing sounds, sending shivers down my spine.

CHAPTER 5

I HAD ALWAYS been ashamed of knowing Burl Higgins by name and of the fact that he knew me by mine. Burl was a hellion's hero, the town untouchable, and as a hired fieldhand he was unpardonable. It was near quitting time the next day when a police car drove up our lane with Burl Higgins in it. A policeman brought Burl to our back doorstep dressed in a pauper's discards, which included an oversized jacket and jeans to the other extreme.

Mr. Pearl and I were returning to the barn from the field. When we saw the policeman and Burl, Mr. Pearl didn't move an inch with interest, but I could not resist listening. I moved closer behind a tree to hear what had brought Burl to kneel before Father's sympathies.

"John, do you know this boy?" the policeman asked Father after Father had calmly walked to the house from the field.

"What have you done, Burl?" Father looked at Burl, who wasn't looking at anyone.

"Burl's been involved in another car accident," the policeman said. "This time the damage amounts to three hundred dollars on the other driver's car."

Burl's only reaction was to smile. He was twisted like his humor—always grinning, always laughing at the wrong things.

"Is it funny, son?" The policeman's tone of voice changed from an official monotone to something more threatening. "I can take you to the city jail and let you laugh for a few days." The tips of

Burl's smile immediately straightened, and I heard him mumble something about not being anybody's son.

"Why did you bring Burl to me?" Father asked. "I'm not responsible for his behavior when he's not working in my fields."

This time Burl spoke. The words slid out lazily. "I need to borrow the money, boss. If I don't pay up, they'll keep my car."

"That's at least two months' work at your pace." Father's voice sounded too soft for my satisfaction. I stood behind the maple tree fuming. I wanted to shout, "Lock him up and throw away the key!" But then Burl turned his queer stare on me and made me want to disappear. I took off my asthma mask self-consciously.

"I'll work hard, boss," Burl said with false sincerity. "Could have happened to anyone." I rolled my eyes with disgust and he spied it. He glared at me and I glared back brazenly.

"That car of yours violates every safety rule that exists." The policeman smiled cynically at Burl, who merely yawned. "It's a distraction to other drivers."

Then the policeman took out a piece of paper from his heart pocket and began reading the most disgraceful account of the major flaws in Burl's automobile.

"No muffler," he began, "a rope for a clutch, no windshield wipers, no rear-view mirrors—or rear window—no turn signals, one cardboard side window, and rusty steel springs sticking up out of the back seat cushions. We found twenty-three empty whiskey bottles in the back seat, and he's underage."

"You ain't got no proof I drank a drop of it." Burl perked up his head for the first time.

"We also found a rat living in his glove compartment."

"Ain't no law against having pets in the car." Burl acted wise.

"Burl also says he doesn't have an address," the policeman said.

"I thought you were living in that miner's shack at the old Tri-K mine." Father was not the least surprised by any of Burl's calamities or by the condition of Burl's car. He had listened patiently to both parties with a twinkling of humor in his eyes.

"We was. The shack burned down. Me and Amos been living in my car."

"Who's this Amos?" The policeman looked surprised at the mention of another person's name.

"Amos is my rat." Burl looked at the policeman with tight-drawn eyes.

FATHER WENT INSIDE the house to write a check. When he returned, he told Burl to report to work the following day regardless of the weather. When the policeman took Burl away, there was a smirk of accomplishment on Burl's foreboding face. Father's heart was in the right place. He was convinced that everyone needed a chance and that he was the only one who could give that chance to Burl. But the sight of Burl slumped down in the back seat of the squad car, his eyes staring off into some sick space, made me imagine the worst.

Burl and I had had our arguments the summer before, as he specialized in sneaking long naps in the tall weeds, stretched out like a lean wild cat with one foot propped upon his knee. On many an afternoon I had not resisted the temptation of picking up large dirt clods and hitting him in the pit of his stomach while he dozed, at which time he would jump to his feet and growl through his teeth. Then he would angrily strangle some invisible neck of space with his hands, which is all I ever stayed to see.

Father and Mr. Pearl seemed blind to Burl's faults, even when I expressed to them in no uncertain terms that Burl hated Tippy Ten and me with a serious passion. They were protective of Burl and his past, except for revealing the fact that his family was dead and that a few years before Burl had terrorized the teachers at the city high school until they signed a safety petition to permanently dismiss him.

I saw Burl's evil as two kinds, with the more dangerous evil being hidden by the apparent bad manners, bad language, and lazy indifference to life. If Burl had cleansed his wounds while sweating in the fields, hated his birth, or cursed the land, I would have sensed some hope for him, for these were the common complaints of fieldhands. But there seemed to be no regret in Burl, just an absence of pain. There was nothing common about a boy who never cried with his words, movements, or eyes, and even an adolescent could see that Burl had never known the urge.

Mr. Pearl was making baskets when I moped back to the barn, my heart dragging. Father walked in soon after with a good-natured grin on his face.

"Burl's got himself into trouble again." He directed his words to Mr. Pearl and half-laughed.

"It isn't funny!" I said. "You'll never get your money's worth out of Burl Higgins." I was thinking of all the things three hundred dollars could buy.

Father ignored my comment and moved to the back of the barn. Mr. Pearl followed soon after, and when Father mounted the tractor and started the engine, the two men talked. Despite the roar of the motor, I heard Burl's name mentioned twice. The barn shifted its weight just then with a gust of wind and I thought of the secrets of two grown whispering men. If the old barn could talk, it would surely tell all of them. So I waited to see if Mr. Pearl would mention Burl to me.

Finally Father backed the tractor out of the barn and Mr. Pearl returned to his basket stacking. I began tending to Puddin, pretending disinterest in the conversation they had just finished.

"Maybe your little friend would like some rye seed," Mr. Pearl said. He opened a cobweb-covered storage cabinet and pulled out a burlap pouch. Puddin had been my captive for nearly a week, but was definitely a contented little prisoner. I was attempting to teach him to walk on my hands, while Tippy Ten pouted from a safe distance with jealous eyes.

"Good dog," Mr. Pearl praised Tippy for his priestly patience. "Tippy Ten ain't no dumb animal." At the mention of his name, Tippy Ten swept the dirt floor with his bushy tail and scooted an inch closer.

"Stay, Tippy," I reminded him.

"You're going to have that pigeon dancin' before the day's end," Mr. Pearl chuckled.

"We'll all be dancing to the tune of the devil with Burl Higgins working here. He'll ruin my summer, you wait! He's as mean as a spotted snake. And his bad language will wilt the cabbage."

Burl's tongue was taboo on our place. His vocabulary had consisted mostly of four-letter words until Father insisted that Burl use cleaner substitutes when he expressed his filthy thoughts. Otherwise Burl couldn't keep his job. He had acted haughty at first; cursing was a hard habit for him to break. Sometimes Burl's tongue would slip, then he'd quickly mend it in the middle, like, "I got the da-dern tractor started boss, but I cut my finger on that da-dern cable. That tractor ain't worth sh-sugar." Of course Burl never bothered about his profanity when he talked under his breath, which is what he did mostly.

"Give the boy credit for something. At least he tries to improve his bad language." Mr. Pearl smiled in spite of his scolding.

"I'm not giving him credit for a thing. Burl bothers me the way the dead haunt the living. Doesn't Burl bother you?" Still, I wanted to know why Father and Mr. Pearl defended him so. Perhaps Burl had threatened them into liking him.

"Burl don't bother me none." Mr. Pearl steadily stacked his baskets. His face muscles never flinched. "You're thinkin' bad before bad happens. He ain't ever touched you, has he?" His words sat on the fringes of concern.

"Not yet. But he gives me the uneasies. Haven't you ever seen his eyes? It's evil the way he uses them. Like he's looking at the world through a piece of rusty pipe." I narrowed my vision precisely. "And when my back is turned, I can feel his eyes on me like a thousand little hooks sticking in my skin." Just then Puddin walked up my arm, his claws creating the same sensations as Burl's sinister stares.

"Nobody has eyes like that except in that overactive imagination of yours." Mr. Pearl laughed, a bit relieved at what seemed to be exaggerations.

"Imagination, huh!" I put Puddin back in the crate and secured the knot lock that I had fashioned from rope.

"Ada, Burl's evil is innocent." Mr. Pearl defended him like a country lawyer. "Don't try to understand it; just remember it and don't harbor hate for him."

"Remember it? Don't worry. I'll never forget a stupid thing like that. If Burl's evil is innocent, then this pigeon's a peacock. Come on Puddin, let's see you spread those beautiful feathers." I guffawed as the pigeon nodded and gawked.

"I'm saying that Burl wasn't lucky enough to have kin to care for him. He ain't had any upbringing. Have you ever seen that two-headed tree by Pigeon Pond? The tree that's limbs grow sideways instead of up?"

"Sure. The tree that the Indians shaped so they'd know it was beside a buffalo watering hole. The tree with the heart cut out of it."

"That's the one. Well, Burl's a lot like that two-headed tree. Those Indians pruned that tree when it was just a seedling so it would grow that way. And when Burl was just a baby, somebody or something provoked him so that he grew apart from the ways of common folks instead of upright. His rights and wrongs ain't the same as ours, so we got to tend to him the best way we can. Instead of being a freak of nature, like some trees that lightning strikes or the wind bends, Burl and that two-headed tree are freaks by the hands of man."

"I still think he's a lost cause. And just because he's an orphan or worse doesn't mean he can't hurt people or things. I think you like Burl better than me. Dad's partial to him too. You're both always defending him."

Mr. Pearl laughed. "You silly girl." He threw back his head, his laughter carrying beyond the barn beams that housed sparrow nests and supported the slanting roof. "You silly, silly girl."

CHAPTER 6

I DID NOT KNOW what I longed for, only that I longed for more. I could not contain all myself. As I grew that spring, the gaps grew until there were places for loneliness to slip in, lonely places that the old could not fill.

I could not recall a time when I hadn't been satisfied with Mr. Pearl's companionship. The time I spent with other acquaintances could have been compared to the amount of pennies children collect in a jar and donate to the poor, the contents of which could buy little but would be worth many a sincere wish. And wishes had a way of changing things; hidden wishes were the seeds of dreams.

How spring twisted and stained the senses! The very next morning I walked to the woods before the sun was quite up. The wild violets were plentiful in the grass, and deep in the woods they dwelt beneath twigs and earth cracks. They grew where the sun was only a shadow, and they drank the dimness to make their colors a richer purple. I planned to carry the violets with me to school that day so that I would be closer to what they were and from where they came.

I thought about the angel as I walked. I always thought about the angel; every other second I was remembering it, and I was wishing that I could be free of myself, that I could fly. I was wishing to see the angel when I heard the strange sound.

I moved closer to the sound. I knew that it couldn't be a field-hand at that early hour. But someone with a shovel was disturbing the stubborn ground in the exact spot the angel had been seen.

45

I moved closer, beside the pine break where twelve tall pines marked the boundary between the Bell Farm and Father's property. And then I saw her. I moved closer and hid behind bushes and mist and spied upon the strangest girl with a shovel in her hand. She was bending with the shovel, then stooping with it.

"This can't be! This can't be!" she was chanting as the dirt flew around her.

Finally, after a few furious minutes, she flung the shovel aside and scooped the dirt away with her bare impatient hands. From what I could see with her back to me more often than not, she was a stranger. When she did manage to turn in my direction her wide worried eyes were haunting. Her face was like porcelain and her hair was red and a bit wavy.

"Ouch! Oh!" She picked a stiff pine needle out of her thumb.

"Oh Caesar!" she yelped again. Another pine needle stuck her pale skin and she shook her hand to shake off the pain.

I wanted to help her, more from curiosity than kindness, but I kept silent. In the muted light, she was like a painting come to life. I'm sure she didn't suspect I was watching. Once a rabbit rustled some undergrowth close to where I stood hiding and she froze with fear, listening until she saw the rabbit hop. Then relief revived her and she continued to dig.

"You've got to be here! This isn't happening!" She was breathless and losing her energy.

She picked up the shovel again and finally, after digging at least ten holes and finding nothing, her shovel struck something hard. I leaned closer to see what she had buried valuable enough to be uncovered at dawn on a weekday. She fell to her knees again and then, panic stricken, she put her entire head into a hole. For a moment I lost sight of her from the neck up. Then she lifted her head and reached into the hole, only to pull out a hollow soup bone. The bone did not suit her and, as she threw it down, she burst into tears.

"Oh my beautiful . . . Oh my pretty . . . Oh no no no no no no." She crawled from hole to hole moaning.

Her spirit shriveled before me from an uncontrollable temper to the broken bleats of a little lamb. When she tried to speak again, her lips quivered incoherently. Dirt had accumulated on her chin, forehead, and nose. Painstakingly, she cupped her hands as if suddenly her fortune would take shape from the dirt that covered them. But then her anger returned. She smacked her palms together and rubbed them on her skirt before plopping herself down in the midst of her little mounds of sorrow looking lost and abandoned.

By this time the fog was lifting and another rabbit ran into the bushes beside me. I jerked back my head to hide, but I wasn't quick enough. She saw me move, and every muscle of her body stiffened. A curtain of fog was my only defense, but the fog could not camouflage enough of me to save her surprise.

"God help me!" she managed to shout as she jumped to her feet, kicked up her heels, and ran toward the Bell Farm.

It wasn't any wonder that she lost her wits. Only then did I realize that I was wearing my asthma mask, which must have looked grotesque and ghostly in the fog and mist. I tore the mask off and threw it into the weeds.

BURL REPORTED TO WORK that same morning to begin paying off his debts to Father, adding misery to the mystery of the stranger in the pine row. His jalopy snarled and spit oil until he finally stopped it by the barn. I was sitting on the back step waiting for Mrs. Moulton when Burl walked up in all his audacity.

"Where's your false face, ugly?" He tore off a dandelion leaf that was growing between our sidewalk slabs and held it close to my nose, trying to torment a wheeze out of me.

"Give up, Burl," I said. "Save your energy for pacing in your cell at the jailhouse." My expression was poised above reproach.

"You can save yours for the devil," he snarled as he threw down the leaf and made a ritual out of smashing it with his boot. Burl's boots were a few sizes too big. The soles were separating from the turned-up toes, and the heels were uneven and worn from Burl's poor posture. Burl was constantly leaning against any convenient object strong enough to hold his weight. It was a wonder that he didn't get lockjaw from walking around with dirty nails sticking into the bottoms of his feet and from living in a car with rusty steel springs that would more than likely surprise his tail bone at any time.

"Get your old man!" Burl put his hands on his hips.

"It's Mr. Kross to you, Burl. Get him yourself," I said without looking at him. Burl kicked the step to show his contempt, and I ignored him. This time Burl bent down close to my neck, breathing like a sick calf.

"Ugly, I told you to get your old man."

"And I told you to get him yourself." I kept myself steady and calm, but I was beginning to sweat when Mrs. Moulton's car drove up the lane. As we drove away, I heard Burl pounding on the back door, probably wishing it was my head.

CHAPTER 7

"ADA, WHY DON'T YOU extend a helpful hand of friendship to Freddie Moulton?" Mr. Pearl tried to be a peacemaker. "Be nice to him, Ada. What's it going to hurt?"

"It hurts me to be nice to him. It hurts," I said.

But a good deed could be a disguise for revenge. So, I told Mrs. Moulton that Father said Freddie needed a job. It was a perfect plan. With Freddie and Burl at each other's throats, I would have peace at last.

Mrs. Moulton had responded exactly as I had hoped. By the time she picked us up that afternoon after school, she had already made a special trip to town and purchased three pairs of king-sized overalls and a giant lunch box with Paul Bunyan's picture on it for Freddie's convenience. But I didn't have time to warn Father of what I'd done. The minute she stopped the car in my driveway, she jumped out and cornered Father before I could prepare an explanation for anyone.

"John, this is just an inspiration. Freddie needed this job more than anything." By this time Freddie had climbed out of the car and was standing submissively beside her. "The money he earns will pay for his sweets and toys. This is exactly what he needs." She patted Freddie's shoulder now and then as she rambled on. Father gave me one of his melting looks and I knew that he knew exactly what I had done.

"Freddie has promised to work his hardest, and the fresh air will be beneficial to him." Mrs. Moulton's tongue wagged nonstop. "He's been so peaked lately. Just tell me when you want him."

"I'll call you," Father managed to say.

Mrs. Moulton pulled the king-sized overalls our of a sack that she carried with her. "Do you think these are appropriate, Mr. Kross? I want Freddie to look like the other workers."

"That's fine, Mrs. Moulton." Father put his hand to his mouth, concealing a slight smile. I was glad to see his sense of humor hadn't left him.

"Thank, Mr. Kross, for the job." Mrs. Moulton gave Freddie a nudge with her elbow.

"Thank you," Freddie grunted. Then, like a little whirlwind, Mrs. Moulton led Freddie back to the car, chattering to the thin air. I knew Father wanted to discuss the matter with me immediately, but Mr. Pearl drove up on the tractor. He was having trouble with the plow adjustment and needed all of Father's attention. I somehow knew Father was looking forward to talking to me at dinner.

At the dreaded hour, Father seemed himself, smiling regardless of his daughter's hiring practices.

"You've been out early the last few mornings, Ada." Father shook the salt shaker, seasoning the store-bought tomatoes. His face was pink from the spring sun.

"Just yesterday morning," I said, knowing he was about to make his move, "I went out to pick wild violets."

"Where are they?" Mother loved them as much as I.

"I—I changed my mind." I was tempted to share the experience in the mist for a distraction, but I decided to keep the story of the girl with the shovel to myself for a time.

"Ada hasn't got time to sleep," Father said. "She's too busy hiring my help for me. Ada, are you going to pay for all the vegetables Freddie eats on the job? He'll do more damage than all the tomato worms I've got."

"Maybe not, Dad. He'll work as hard as Burl Higgins."

"That's another worry." Father rubbed his forehead. "He'll

persecute Freddie. Remember what he did to the Wessel boy last summer? Stole the pants right off the boy and left him in the field to hide until dark." Father had to laugh. I had forgotten about that incident.

"Burl doesn't get along with anyone." I thought of that very morning on the step. "He's bothering me already."

"I told you last year, Ada, to ignore the boy and he'll leave you alone. When you smart off to him it agitates his temper. Anyway, you shouldn't be out in the fields bothering the help."

"For your information, Burl goes out of his way to bother me!" I felt my ears burning. Burl had only been to work one day, and I was already defending myself on both sides of the fence.

"Well, John," Mother said. "If Freddie isn't a good worker, at least you'll know that you tried to help him." Mother walked over to Father and kissed the top of his head, embarrassing him with her influence. She quickly cleared the table.

"I don't have any choice, do I?" Father said. "I couldn't say no to Mrs. Moulton after she had invested money in Freddie's work wardrobe. You should have seen her, Emily, standing by the barn holding overalls bigger than Pearl's and mine together." Some of Father's disgust was released in laughter.

"I'm sorry for the whole mess." I knew apologizing was useless.

"Well, Ada. I'm going to make you personally responsible for Freddie's welfare while he's working here. Is that understood?"

"Yes, sir." I would rather have had a spanking or a good tongue lashing. A hard hand would have shaken some of the guilt off of my shoulders, but since it wouldn't be applied I knew I would have to spend my summer paying for every mistake Freddie made, knowing that they stemmed from mine.

"FREDDIE MOULTON," I SAID, "if you're going to work for Father, the first rule is that nothing goes into your mouth that you do not carry in your lunch bucket." Freddie and I were standing on the sidewalk in front of Mount Mercer Private School the next day, waiting for his mother.

"Ada, what are you trying to say?" He glared at me through his glasses.

"I'm telling you, no free sampling. Do you understand that?"

"I understand, but you just remember, Ada Kross, that you got me this miserable little job and it would serve you right if I ate plants and all!"

"Freddie, I'm telling you for your own good. You'll get sick and die. Your eyes are bigger than your stomach."

"Ada, you're making fun of my eyes." He took a step forward as if he could threaten me with his size.

"You idiot. I'm not making fun of your silly eyes."

"See?" He stomped his foot.

"Freddie, just make sure you earn your money. That's all I've got to say."

"Ada Kross, I didn't want a job. I was planning on sitting by the lake and sunning all summer. Now I'm going to be out with weeds and bugs and dirty-looking fieldhands."

"What do you mean by that?" I doubled up my fist. "How would you like me to bust your big balloon? I'll knock that hot air right out of you! Don't you ever let me hear you say another word about fieldhands being dirty, because dirty is being fat and sloppy and lazy like you."

Freddie began to blubber. He took off his glasses and tried to wipe the tears away. "Ada, if you knew how much I hate you, you'd hurt. You'd hurt just from knowing how much I hate you. And if you knew how ugly you look, you'd even get uglier just from knowing that, too. If you weren't a girl, I'd sock you."

"Don't let that stop you!"

"Where'd you get all them mean-looking cinders in your knees? Golly goodness, they're ornery lookin' little cuts." Mr. Pearl and I were resting beneath the pin oaks after quitting time.

"Freddie Moulton pushed me down today. We had it out, and he's heavy enough to move a truck. God Almighty knows that I hope he dies from sunstroke the first day he works for us."

"Ada, hush."

"He called me a skinny, ugly runt again. I wanted to pop him, and I was ready to, but he pushed me first and ran, the cowardly buffalo. Ouch!" I was using a needle to remove the remaining cinders.

"Ada, calm down so that my food can digest. I tell you you're always fumin' and fightin' over somethin'."

"He's going to work for Dad, but don't worry. He won't last three days. He's scared of boys I consider sissified. One look at Burl and that fat'll fly! Ouch!"

"Did you sterilize that needle?"

"Of course. I spit on it." I had developed an expertise at cinder removal. I had it down to a science, my best removal time being a cinder per minute provided that the cinders were not in my backside.

"How's it going to look on Sunday for a pretty young girl to have cinders in her knees?"

"Now who's going to look at these knees? They're as bony as knots on a tree."

"Goodness, but your legs are longer than the legs of a young fawn." Mr. Pearl yawned as if he found studying them exhausting. I stretched my legs, and my feet did seem farther away. The lines and shape of them curved in and out instead of being boyishly straight as I remembered them.

"Do you think I should wear white socks still . . .?" It was the fashion of the day for young ladies to wear white nylon anklets, and a must at Mount Mercer School.

"What color of socks do you want to wear?" Mr. Pearl looked at me quizzically.

"I don't want to wear white socks. I want to wear silk stockings."

"Ada, am I hearing you rightly? You want to wear silk stockings with cinders in your knees?"

"Did Sweet Cindy wear silk stockings? I bet she did, didn't she?"

"She did. But she was a full-grown woman."

"Well, I'm a full-grown woman in my legs. I do believe that they won't grow another inch. It's just the rest of me that has to catch up with them."

"Ada, I thought you didn't want to become a woman. You sure confuse me."

"You're just as confusing." I pulled his hat down over his eyes by the brim.

"All right. Who've you seen wearing silk stockings?"

"The neighbor girl. I saw her wearing them one morning when I hid in the bushes."

"Ada, why hide from her? Introduce yourself. She's probably as scared of you as you are of her."

"That's the truth." I explained to him about the morning in the mist when I had mortified her with my mask.

"I think she'd like you anyway," he said.

"I don't know what to do." I was unrehearsed at making friends, as Mr. Pearl, up until then, had been my only lasting one.

I began watching her every afternoon as she stepped off the Eagle Creek school bus. I was home half an hour earlier, so I could find a good place to hide and she never suspected I was close by.

One afternoon she looked happy, with a contented smile upon her face. The next afternoon she was angry and kicked stones up her lane. On Friday she recited poetry with an accent that was most entertaining, and later that evening I heard piano music coming from her house. I sat in the dark where the blue-bells met the field and through the window I watched her at the piano. Those same industrious hands that dug mysterious holes played classical concertos.

CHAPTER 8

BY THE FIRST WEEK IN MAY the fields began to blossom and there was work to be done everywhere in the garden. Freddie was called to work the next day, a Saturday. I felt obligated to stand by and watch over him, and also to keep a close eye on Burl. I was prepared for anything.

Burl came to work, turning his car engine off halfway up our lane and letting it coast into an elm tree to stop. Before his traffic mishap Burl's car had appeared to be a typical trash heap, but that Saturday morning it looked gaudier than a tattoo on a baby. Burl had ransacked the city dump and found a clear bubble dome that had once covered the cockpit of an obsolete airplane, and that fit perfectly over the spot where the convertible top once had been. Burl added to this attraction by wearing a ten-gallon hat that would have been a scavenger's deluxe item if it hadn't looked so horrendous on him.

Father was fairly amused, but he walked over to examine the tree. When Mother looked out of the kitchen window to investigate the crash, I motioned for her to come out and get a better look. She slammed the screen door behind her and walked toward me, laughing and comparing the sight of it to something out of the funny papers.

"I'm ashamed of that hideous car and him," I said when she was standing beside me. "It looks like a madman's car."

"Ada, that car isn't hurting anything. Someday you'll look back on this incident and laugh."

"What about that tree?" I said. "Not even a tree can take too many jolts like that."

"I hope Burl doesn't make a habit of it," she admitted.

Mr. Pearl drove up about then in his pickup truck. Hank and Abe had hitched a ride with him, and the three of them climbed out.

"If that don't beat all," Mr. Pearl said. He gave a lengthy whistle as he walked over to Burl's car and examined the new top. "Some conversation piece you got there, Burl."

"That's something else." Hank was impressed with the looks of it. He had the same deteriorated taste as Burl, who was so proud that he spit in his hand and wiped one of many dirt spots off of the bubble dome.

"I'm getting sick just watching him," I said in pure protest. "It's a sin to be so stupid."

"Ada!" Mother said. "It's a sin to have so much hate inside you. I've never heard you talk so hateful about anyone. You better pray for forgiveness."

"For Burl or for me?" I pretended to block out the sun by shielding my eyes with my hand, but actually it was her look of reproach that I was avoiding. She finally walked away, shaking her head as if to say, "I give up."

When Freddie arrived, he crawled out of the car, appearing stiff and neat in his new work clothes. He waved to his mother with solemn eyes. Burl didn't notice Freddie with everybody paying attention to his vehicle, and I was relieved when Father separated Freddie and Burl two fields apart. Freddie hoed cabbage, and Burl planted stake tomatoes with Rexy, Abe, Hank, and Mr. Pearl.

The trouble started shortly before noon, when Freddie knocked politely on our back door, complaining that he didn't want to use the outhouse that Father had provided for the help. Mother was flustered at first, but finally agreed to let him come in and use our facilities. Burl was watching it all from the tomato patch and when Freddie walked out, Burl fired his first insults.

"Hey, Hippo," Burl called from the field as Freddie passed him on his way back to the cabbage patch. Freddie didn't answer, but continued walking.

"Hey, Hippo. Don't walk when I'm talking to you." Freddie, in all his stupidity, stopped.

"Huh?" Freddie looked around to see where the strange voice was coming from. "You talkin' to me?"

"What's the matter, Hippo? Are you afraid of the flies?" Burl yelled it this time.

"Huh?" Freddie looked bewildered.

"Hey, boys, Hippo uses the boss's john." Burl's voice was in its height of glory.

"John who?" Freddie said quite earnestly.

"Whoooooooooooeeeeeeeeeee! John who, he says. John who?" Burl threw his hat into the air at the same time the noon whistle blew.

The fieldhands dropped their hoes and marked their spots before they headed for the shadiest places to eat lunch. I walked out to the barn to feed Puddin, not expecting to be surrounded by the enemy.

"Where'd your old man get that Hippo?" Burl mumbled with his mouth full. Burl, Abe, and Hank were sitting on bushel baskets eating their sandwiches without washing their dirty, green-tomato-stained fingers.

"Mind your own business, Burl." I took Puddin out of its cage, his leg still tied to the twine, and let him stand on the top of my hand.

"He's bigger than a da-dern hippo, ain't he?" Burl laughed between chews.

"You shouldn't talk. You belong in a zoo yourself." I made a practice not to look at Burl. I acted preoccupied with my bird.

"Why you takin' Hippo's part? Is he your heart's desire?" Burl looked over at Hank. "Hank, I do believe Ada's got herself a boyfriend—a hippo-potamus."

"I've always wanted to see a hippo," Hank said. "This is the closest I ever come to seeing one." Hank loved to play along, talking and looking as inferior as ever. I fed Puddin seed by seed, acting unamused.

"He's your secret love, ain't he?" Burl directed his words to me. "Ain't that cute? Well, just you wait, Ada. Him and me are going to get along like you never seen. That hippo with his kewpie-doll eyes." Burl then slugged an entire bottle of cola down at one time, making obnoxious gulping sounds while Hank and Abe cackled.

"Freddie's not my sweetheart. He's as big a misfit as you. But I'll tell you one thing." I felt a lie swell up in me. "Freddie could lick you with his kewpie-doll eyes closed. He's a wrestler."

"You're lying, Ada," Burl said. "You da-dern little liar. I'll bet you a switching that I can beat him."

"I don't gamble with criminals. Especially criminals who don't have good enough manners to eat in a barn. And don't let me see you messing around my pigeon's cage or you'll regret it." I put Puddin back in its crate.

"Ever hear a da-dern pigeon squawk?" Burl said to Hank loud enough for me to feel the strain of listening. I leaned in their direction.

"Nope. I can't say that I have," Hank answered, pretending an interest.

"Sh-shoot, all you got to do is pull their da-dern tail feathers one at a time." Burl moved his fingers to demonstrate, and by that time my eyes were focused on his melodramatic performance.

"See this sign? It reads 'NO TRESPASSING.' " I pointed to a sign I had painted so that Puddin's melon crate wouldn't be mistaken for an empty one. "In other words, Burl, hands off or else! You're already in hot water, and if your touch my pigeon I'll make sure that hot water boils."

"You couldn't melt an icicle, Miss High and Mighty, let alone cook my goose," Burl laughed and looked at me from the top of my head to the soles of my feet.

"How do you know this stinking pigeon wants to be your private property?" Hank was acting snooty.

I didn't answer because I didn't know. It was obvious I was outnumbered, not by brains, but by meanness, so I tied the sign to the pigeon's cage to make it legal and I left the barn.

"THAT NEW BOY'S got the movingest eyes," I heard Hank say as I walked through the tomato patch that afternoon to visit with Mr. Pearl. Hank paused from his planting to watch Freddie walk from the water hose to the cabbage patch for the tenth time. "Makes me dizzy just to look at them wigglin'."

"Well, at least he ain't swearing he saw an angel," Abe said. He leaned on his hoe handle and looked in Mr. Pearl's direction. "Now, that's real eye trouble, if you ask me."

My heart skipped a beat. I walked faster toward Mr. Pearl, who was working not far from their cruelty.

"Who's asking you?" Rexy said. She was father's only woman fieldhand and was twice as rugged as most men. Rexy was soft for Mr. Pearl because, after all those years of working together, he still tipped his hat to her and treated her like royalty.

"It bugs the heck out of me," Hank said, "all this nonsense 'bout heaven and that glory angel that came glidin' down in that field like the sun. Hallelujah! I done seen the light!" Hank held up his hands in false praise.

"Don't mock God, boy," Rexy said in a voice as gruff as her rough exterior. Her bandana-bedecked head rose above the others like a red flag.

"Do you mean you believe that Pearl saw an angel right in this here field?" Hank asked her.

I saw Mr. Pearl's jaw tighten.

"I ain't sayin' I believe him, but I ain't sayin' I don't," Rexy said. "Just shut your trap and move your muscles like you're supposed to, before I call the boss."

"Well, I say the old man needs his brain restuffed with a little chicken manure. Then he'll see things like the rest of us," Abe said.

"Don't listen to them, Mr. Pearl," I said. "They're dumber than weed roots."

Mr. Pearl continued to hoe.

"The old man's crazy," Abe shouted it for Mr. Pearl's benefit.

"I believe Pearl thinks he seen an angel," Rexy said. "Pearl don't know nothin' more than what he sees 'cause he can't read or write. So, if he sees something like that, you know he ain't read it from some fancy book of fairy tales."

"And what he saw, he saw. You jackasses!" I shouted to the boys. Then I turned to Mr. Pearl again.

"Don't listen to them. They're low-bellied snakes crawling in the garden of Eden. Doomed—all of them."

"Calm down, Ada." Mr. Pearl swallowed hard.

"Tomorrow, we'll read about the angel in the Bible again. Your favorite part: 'lest you dash your foot against a stone.' "

"No need, Ada. You know we got it memorized."

"There's a lot more passages about angels we haven't touched. We haven't been reading the Good Book like we should." I was close to tears, fearing his discouragement.

"I suppose we could." He snorted in some dust. His face was poised despite the strain from those uncivilized tongues.

"Well, we won't let another day pass until we've studied some," I said.

"It gets me through." His hoe hit a stone. He bent down to pick it up and examined it before tossing it away.

"It weren't no angel," Hank bellowed. "It was Peter Rabbit hippity-hoppity in his little white suit. You done seen the Easter bunny, Mr. Pearl."

"Why, look over there! It's an angel! Look at it!" Abe pointed to Rexy. "Ain't it bee-u-ti-ful."

"Abe, if you don't tighten your tongue . . ." Rexy said. "You wouldn't know an angel if you stepped on one, which you won't, 'cause you're going to hoe the devil's crab grass for sure. Get on with your work and let this angel business be."

I picked up a rock the size of my fist. "I'm going to put Hank out of his sinful misery," I said to Mr. Pearl.

"Ada, put it down. Don't go fighting with boys twice your size," he answered.

"I'm not going to fight him. I'm going to . . ."

"I'm leavin' for a time. Promised your daddy I'd plow the southeast field. Now calm yourself. Come away from this tomato patch," Mr. Pearl said.

"Holy, holy, holy!" Hank shouted like a fanatic.

"Holy, holy, holy!" Abe chimed in, spreading his arms like wings.

"I hope God strikes both of you dead." I nearly spit. Mr. Pearl was walking away, serenely enough not to look like a coward or a fool. My heart wrestled with its vows of belief. All this suffering for seeing such a beautiful thing. I wanted wrath and destruction for those nonbelievers. "I'm going to do my best to get both of you fired!" I shouted. "You're both as worthless as fly turd. If I hear another word, I'm docking you both an hour's wage."

"I'm so sc-scared." Hank pretended to shake. "I don't believe a word of it. What about you, Burl, do you believe it?"

"I believe nothin'." He looked at me as if I were less than that. "Hey, ugliness. Where's your muzzle?" His voice was slow and lazy as ever. I threw back my head royally and pretended that his insults could not offend me. "How'd you grow to be so ugly, Ada?"

"You're such a mole, Burl," I said as I walked toward the edge of the tomato patch.

"I'm a what?" Burl bit his lower lip, showing his chipped front tooth.

"A mole. A filthy, scroungy mole." I continued walking.

"You're asking for it, you da-dern little . . ." He took a step closer.

"Go dig a hole!"

"Don't listen to him, honey." Rexy stood up. "Burl don't know nothin' 'bout what's pretty." She stepped over to Burl. "Get busy, you numbskull."

Burl laughed mechanically.

"Rexy, I don't listen to Burl," I said. "Everybody knows he's so ugly his face could crack concrete. You know all those cracks in our sidewalks? Well, all those cracks, Burl looked at!"

Snickers sprouted on all sides of us. Burl retaliated by clomping toward me from his plant row. He stopped in front of me, casually blocking my path.

"Look at those da-dern pigeon toes." He shook his head and I quickly glanced at my feet. Once I had recovered from his insult, I stepped to one side in an attempt to move past him, but he blocked my way. "And them bird legs. Ain't it a shame. Got bird legs too. Ever see such bird legs, boys?"

"Why, they're skinnier than chicken bones." Hank bent over slightly, exaggerating an interest. He glanced at Burl for approval, then looked back at me. "Here chick chick. Here chick chick."

By this time Abe was practically stumbling from laughter and Burl had provoked smiles from the others, except for Rexy.

"I said, 'Go dig a hole.' " This time I raised my voice ferociously across the field.

"By the way," Burl sneered, his face looking like a date. "You ever seen a rat take after a bird?"

"Burl, if you touch my pigeon I'll—" I turned and faced him, clenching my flimsy fist.

"You'll what? Ain't you a toughy? Ain't she a toughy, boys?" Burl spit out the end of a weed he was chewing. "You know what you need, Ada? You need a good hard switchin'." He grabbed my arm in a wrench's hold and, still holding on to me, tore off a switch from a dead limb. He pulled me toward the tree row away from everybody.

"You need a good bath," I said. I wanted to cry and scream. "That's what you need."

"Yep, you need a good hard switchin', and nobody can give you a switchin' like that 'cept me."

Burl pulled me to the pines against my will. I was close to crying out for help and admitting defeat when the pine branches shook and spread and a red head popped up between the skirt of needles.

"She needs nothing of the kind! You snake in the grass! You degenerate!"

To me her appearance was as miraculous as when the Almighty parted the Red Sea.

"Who the he-heck are you?" Burl dropped my arm, which was red from his grip's imprint.

"Don't ask questions," my rescuer said in my behalf. "You are here only to be told. Disperse this instant, you maggot!"

Burl stepped back and studied this red-headed hot wire without one remark. I'm certain that he would have stayed to take his stand, but I sensed that he thought her to be insane or extremely strange. He flicked at the hair in his eyes and turned around and walked back to his spot in the tomato patch. As for me, I had never heard such elaborate words, all of which described Burl perfectly.

"Glory be. You numbed his pointed tongue," I said to her. "You helped me more than you'll ever know."

"I hope I've put him out of commission permanently. However, his kind usually persists. If you'd like to return the favor, come around on the other side of the trees."

I made my way to the other side and looked at her without any obstruction to my view. She was remarkably lovely, with cool gray eyes and a fresh complexion, as if she had lived in the country longer than I. After we both had time to study each other she spoke, this time more gently.

"I'm in a terrible dilemma. Have you by any chance seen any stray shoes lying around?" She looked hopeful, but when I didn't immediately respond, the look of despair from the morning in the mist returned and clouded her brow.

"What kind of shoes do you mean?" I was expecting a different kind of buried treasure—jewels, old coins, or perhaps mysterious bones—but I would never have guessed shoes to be her obsession.

"My shoe collection. Let's see." Her slight lisp was charming and didn't affect her delivery. "There's the red ones with the princess toes. I know I'll never find another pair like them. And the blue ones with the thin straps that could be worn across the foot or around the ankle." She frowned maturely and wrinkled her forehead, trying to remember. "And the black ones with the dainty bows—all of them very stylish. Oh, if I could perish the thought that they've been stolen."

"Whatever would they be doing out here?" I couldn't believe what I was hearing.

"That's a story too complicated to believe." She handed me the shovel. "But if you could help me dig, I might locate them." She sat down and started digging with her hands. "Oh yes, there are the brown ones with the authentic brass buckles." She sounded out of breath. Still, she tried to explain and dig at the same time. "You see, I wore galoshes to school for an entire week because of the dampness and the cold, and when the weather permitted it, I came back to change into my new spring shoes. But I couldn't find them anywhere. Only the empty boxes."

"But why did you keep such special shoes buried in a place like this?"

She stood up at attention. "Because I didn't want to wear these."

For the first time, I noticed the shoes she was wearing. They were thick-soled, hard leather, round-toed, tied shoes. She pointed to her protruding feet.

"Aren't you impressed? They're prescription shoes, but I call them persecution shoes. The answer to my parents' prayers. You see, I don't have any arches. Flat-footed they call it."

"I'm sorry." I looked directly into her eyes so that she could see my sincerity.

"Don't be. It isn't a disease. Father says five out of every fifty people have the same thing."

"Is that a fact?"

"Yes. But it is a real inconvenience to be flat-footed when you're thirteen." She paused and took a deep breath as if she were in need of the oxygen for energy. "Here's my whole routine. I leave the house every school morning wearing these," she lifted the toe of one homely shoe slightly, "and I catch the school bus wearing those." She pointed to the empty shoe boxes. "Well, at least what was once those."

"Your parents don't understand?" I asked her.

"How could they? They think comfort and durability are more important. They just don't understand how uncomfortable I feel wearing these clodhoppers. Have you ever tried dancing with a boy while wearing prescription shoes?"

"No." I didn't dare tell her that I had not danced with a boy under any circumstances. She was obviously more worldly than I.

"It's like dancing with two bricks on your feet. If I accidentally step on my partner's feet, he might as well sit down for the rest of the evening. I know you think I'm exaggerating, but I weighed myself on a scale, with and without my corrective shoes, and I actually weighed five extra pounds with them on."

"That is discouraging," I agreed.

"I've tried everything to wear them out. I went to the city one afternoon and literally threw them out in the middle of the intersection. I left them there for an hour, but they were only dusty when I retrieved them." She sat down to dig in a different spot. I admired her persistence.

"What will you do now?" I began digging with her shovel, close to where she was digging with her hands.

"Fortunately, I had enough money saved to save me. I bought a new pair this week and I buried them and marked them with little sticks over there." She pointed to a fresh mound outlined in a square. "I'm not taking chances this time. Do you suppose somebody is stealing them?"

"I can't think of anyone who would do such a thing," I said. "After all, a person can only do so much with second-hand shoes, no matter how attractive they are. What size do you wear?"

"Size seven with a triple-A heel."

"Oh." I thought it was a coincidence that she wore the same size as my mother, but I didn't tell her for fear she would be offended by the fact that someone older wore her exact shoe size.

"You'll find them. You've got to," I said cheerily, but deep down I doubted it.

"I don't know. You see," her eyes filled with suspicion, "I saw something dreadful here. I don't want to frighten you, but . . ." She covered her eyes with her soiled hands as if she could blot out the memory of it. "It was a creature of some sort with some kind of horrible deformity; it looked like something from another planet! Oh, I don't know what it was. I'm from the city, and I'm not one to imagine incredible things. But it scared me halfway to heaven and I don't want to meet up with it again."

"Yes, I understand perfectly." I felt my pride surfacing inside; I wasn't about to swallow it and tell her the most unattractive facts about myself.

"You do?" She looked at me and smiled. "Would you be kind enough to watch for shoe prowlers in my shoe hideout?"

"Yes, of course. I'm Ada Kross. We haven't met before this because I go to private school."

"My name is Elizabeth Hathaway Stuckey, but please call me Beth. We just moved here from Cincinnati." She held out her muddy hand and I shook it regardless. "I knew I hadn't seen you on the school bus." She stopped talking and looked toward her house. The dinner bell was clanging in the distance. "I have to go now. It's time for my piano lesson. I'll see you soon, I hope."

"Thanks for defending me against Burl." I had almost forgotten how our conversation had begun. "Come tomorrow if you can."

"I'm glad I was here. When I first heard someone shouting, 'Go dig a hole,' I thought they were talking to me. That was getting too close for comfort."

"That's putting it mildly." I laughed. "Oh Beth?"

"Yes, Ada?"

"Did you hear Burl call me pigeon-toed?" I didn't want her to feel as if she were the only one with something wrong.

"Yes, I heard him."

"Well, I am. I really am."

"Nobody's perfect, Ada. Remember our secret!" She said as she waved and ran, and I was too thrilled to even call out a good-bye.

THAT EVENING AFTER QUITTING TIME Freddie Moulton was missing. I found him at the far end of the cabbage patch, apparently in some pain.

"Oh Ada, I could kill you." His hatred for me made him wince all the more. There were circles of dirt around his eyes and sweat was dripping off the frames of his glasses. "Every muscle in my body is aching."

"Fatty tissue, you mean!" I was low on sympathy.

Freddie started to move. "Ada, I do not have the strength to strangle you, or I would. I can't move. I can't stand up!"

"Well, Freddie, you'll just have to sit in this field all night and be wet with dew and bitten by the wild animals that come out to feed in the fields. Especially the bats!"

"Bats?" Freddie struggled to his feet.

"Yes, bats. Bats bite."

"Ada, you'd like it if I died, wouldn't you? You'd like it if I got eaten up by some animal or if I got bat fever. I'll bat you!"

Freddie moaned when he tried to step toward me. Then he moved stiff-legged toward the house where Mr. Pearl was waiting to take him home.

"Watch those bats!" I shouted after him.

"I'll bat you, Ada. When I can move again, I'm going to . . ."

"Phooey." I laughed out loud. How I loved his misery.

"FLY DROPPINGS! JACKASSES! What kind of daughter am I rearing?" Mother was as hot as the baked beans at dinner. "I did not send you to Sunday school all these years to hear that kind of language shouted across the fields."

"Well, I meant to say, 'dead flies.' But fly turd is more truthful. You didn't send me to Sunday school to learn how to lie, did you? They were making fun of Mr. Pearl and the angel. He never takes his part, so I have to."

"You can't beat those boys at their own wickedness," Father said. "It's time you conducted yourself like a lady."

"There! You admitted it. They are wicked. And today Burl threatened to do perverted things to Puddin, and he mentioned Amos in the process."

"Who's Amos?" Mother asked. Her face was less flushed and she was beginning to relax. She sat at the table and attempted to eat normally.

"Amos is Burl's rat! It lives in his glove compartment."

"I'm sorry I asked." She picked at her food and pushed her salad away.

CHAPTER 9

FATHER SELDOM HAD TIME to rest during the busy spring and summer months, including Sundays, but the next morning he sat in church with Mother and me without a complaint about what he should be home doing. His smooth face reflected the sunlight. He was without wrinkles, except around his temples, and those were ordinary smile-and-squint lines from the sun. Sitting there rather stiffly in his Sunday suit with his hands folded in his lap, he was unblemished, without a thing to hide.

Mother looked especially proud that morning, sitting between Father and me in her pink fitted suit with white ruffles blooming around her face. I felt secure, looking at both of them and listening to the solemn organ music that played while people silently prayed—as if everything I'd ever need was in that room, around and beside me. I had a lot more in my life than an allergy and an asthma mask.

It was while I was thanking the Lord for my new friend, and praying for forgiveness for hating Burl and Freddie, that the organ music stopped and the reverend dropped the bomb.

"Today is the day we honor all mothers," he said, raising his arms in a loving gesture. Mother took hold of my hand, and I could feel all of her warmth inside her glove. My hand felt clumsy holding hers, as if by touching me she would know that I had forgotten what day it was!

I was so ashamed. I realized then why some of the ladies in the congregation were wearing carnation and orchid corsages. By the end of the sermon, "A Mother's Worth," I felt worthless, and I didn't have a voice to sing the last hymn.

Leaving the church, Father greeted friends with his shy almond eyes, and Mother chatted and shook the hands of the visitors. She seemed to be filled with a secret of her own, and, if she knew of my guilt, she didn't act it. All the way home, I sat quietly in the back seat with a confident smile on my face. I'm sure my smile looked convincing, but on the inside of my mouth it felt lopsided and on the verge of quivering.

Once Mother turned to me in the back seat and asked teasingly, "Ada, when do I get my Mother's Day present?" I looked wise and told her, "Soon enough."

From the car, I went directly to Father's desk and grabbed a seed catalog, then ran up to my room, where I cut out a picture of a rose and pasted it onto a folded sheet of paper. I then wrote a poem on the inside:

> This morning is like a rose
> The rose of a sunset
> And you are the best of all roses
> And I am a petal in your garden.
> Thank you for being mine.
> > Love,
> > Your Ada

Downstairs, Mother was fixing Sunday dinner. I carried her card with me into the kitchen, blowing the thick paste dry.

"Mother, I have a little something for you, if you have a minute." I hid the card under the table as I sat down.

"I always have time for a surprise." She sat down beside me, wiping the flour from her fingers with a kitchen towel. "Where is it?" She looked down at the bare table.

"Here," I said almost apologetically, handing her the card. She took it gratefully, and I watched her lovely eyes follow every loop and line of my writing, careful not to miss a word or a meaning. She finished it all too soon.

"This is a beautiful poem, Ada." She kissed me, leaving the scent and the stain of her Sunday lipstick on my cheek.

I felt reassured from the kiss and the compliment that everything was fine, until a tear swam to the side of her eye. Maybe she was remembering a Mother's Day past and my grandmother's sweet face, but she didn't say. She blinked her eyes and wiped a tear away. "I'll keep this lovely card in a special place. Thank you, darling."

She got up from the chair and continued to prepare dinner without expression. The longer I watched her, the less certain I was that she was sad or happy or sentimental. She was too detached to be any of those. But then, while she stirred the soup on the stove, I heard a sigh escape from some sad part of her and I could have sighed ten more from hearing just that one.

She moved about in her stocking feet, pounding the flour into the meat and washing lettuce at the sink. When she sighed by the stove for the second time, I was convinced that she was indeed disappointed in me and I left the kitchen to do something drastic.

There wasn't time for future predictions. Mother's happiness depended on whether Beth Hathaway Stuckey's last surviving pair of shoes still rested where she had buried them. I hated to add to her shoe dilemma, but I would replace the shoes sooner than they would be missed—I hoped.

I hurried to the pine break still wearing my Sunday best, but that didn't stop me from frantically digging once I spotted Beth's stick markers. It was less than a minute before my grimy hands touched the plastic that protected the shoe box. I opened it and inspected the bone-colored shoes. They looked and smelled new enough to pass for a gift. I filled the vacant hole with dirt clods, feeling like a thief and a traitor and praying that I wouldn't be accused as either.

I carried the precious cargo home and tiptoed upstairs to wash my hands which, despite the layer of dirt covering them, smelled of pine sap and smarted from the pricks of the pine needles. I wrapped the box without a bow, feeling not one bit less guilty, but hoping that Mother would believe I had had the present all along.

Mother was standing beside the sink, her tears falling freely, in silent streams down her soft cheeks.

"Mother, don't cry. Why are you crying? Is it because you think I've forgotten you?" I put my arm around her waist to console her. "See." I handed her the wrapped shoe box. "I didn't. Here's a present for you."

"Let's sit down, Ada dear." She took the box from my hand. We both sat down at the kitchen table.

"I have a very special Mother's Day present for you, too." She smiled through sentimental eyes. "Such a beautiful present, that I don't know quite how to tell you. I guess all I can say is—is I'm going to have a baby."

"A baby?" My voice fell an octave. It was one surprise I hadn't been expecting.

"Aren't you happy?" Mother said with a hurt expression.

"Oh yes. Now I won't be so lonely, and Dad may get his son." I said the words slowly. My brain felt numb.

"Your father and I want this baby and we hope that you want it, too. It doesn't matter to us whether it's a girl or a boy. Just as long as it's healthy."

"I wasn't healthy. I'm still not healthy."

"You were healthy, honey. People of all sizes have allergies." She took my cold hand and squeezed it.

"I suppose." I had always wanted a brother and a sister, but everything was happening too fast.

"We won't love you less because we have a new baby," Mother said. "Love isn't like that. When the baby comes, we will all be given more love to give to it—extra love. Of course, you will have to share us and a lot of yourself too. Babies demand a lot of time, but they are beautiful gifts from God. We'll have to decorate the nursery, and you can help me paint your old bassinet and high chair that I've been storing down in the basement. It'll be fun for both of us, and it'll make the time go faster." Her eyes shone. "I was afraid you wouldn't want it."

"Of course I want the baby, too. When is it due?"

"The doctor said about the end of September. I thought you would have noticed my stomach getting a little rounder." She laughed and patted it. "It is, you know. Your father wanted me to wait until today to surprise you, and I hope he isn't disappointed because he wasn't here when I told you."

"I'll be disappointed if you don't open your present." I pointed to the box.

"Oh!" She shook the box. "It couldn't be what it appears to be, could it?" She tore away the paper and opened the shoe box. "It is—it's shoes! Ada, I love them." She slipped them on, raising one foot and then the other, appraising the fit and the style. The gift was worth the trouble for that moment. "They're perfect! I'll wear them over to the Stuckeys today and show Mrs. Stuckey what a thoughtful daughter I have."

"The Stuckeys? What? Why?" My tongue turned to cotton. I was surely cursed.

"While you were upstairs, Mrs. Stuckey called and invited the three of us to their house for dinner. Wasn't that nice? She said that Beth had talked about you so much that they thought we all should get together. We'll be going right after dinner. Why don't you go upstairs and change your dress. It's filthy!"

Our house and the Bell house that the Stuckeys had bought were the oldest houses left on our rural route. They dated back to before Civil War times. Father had often said that if the tallest trees that surrounded the two houses could talk, they could recite more history than a history book could hold.

Both of the two-storied houses were of white weatherboarding, but shaped differently, with styles and settings of their own. My house sat on an obvious hill in the middle of our garden's grounds. The Bell house wasn't as conspicuous. It was hushed and secluded by bushes and sycamore trees that constantly shed pieces of marble bark. Wild blue-bells grew amidst the grass there in early spring. There was a pine garden with paths that led to a fishpond the size of a puddle, an old playhouse, and an outbuilding filled with deserted rabbit hutches. The gray barn was used for a garage. Part of the house was covered with ivy, and there was a holly tree that touched the upstairs windows. I could have painted a picture of the back view of it from memory because of the many times I had passed it on my way to the woods.

When our car stopped at the house, Mr. Stuckey met us on the sidewalk and shook Mother's hand and mine. He was a tall, slightly gray-haired, distinguished man. Mrs. Stuckey walked out and Mr. Stuckey introduced her to us. She looked a lot like Beth, with the same red hair and cool gray eyes. Mrs. Stuckey had a contented air about her and, like the house, she set a peaceful mood.

The men immediately began a conversation about gardening techniques and the chances for rain that week. Mrs. Stuckey led Mother and me into a kitchen with a high ceiling and cabinets that even Father couldn't have reached without a stepladder. It was a room with an echo.

"Where's Beth?" I asked politely, half-hoping she wouldn't appear.

"She's outside somewhere. She'll be back shortly, because I told her dessert would be served as soon as you arrived." Mrs. Stuckey picked up a teapot and carried it with her.

"Your house feels so comfortably cool. Does it have an air conditioner?" Mother asked her.

"No. The secret is that we keep our doors and windows open at night and then close them by day. It keeps the cool air in when we need it. We love this old house already." Mrs. Stuckey smiled with a graceful friendliness when she talked. "I put the dessert on the dining-room table, buffet style, so that we could serve ourselves and sit on more comfortable furniture in the living room," she continued.

"That sounds perfect," Mother said, her new shoes tapping with each step on the kitchen tile. I was tense, just waiting for Beth's entrance. But when the men came in, Beth was not with them.

Mrs. Stuckey decided to start without Beth, and we filled our plates with apple cake, plus mints and nuts. The Stuckeys' living-room decor included an oriental rug and a black upright piano. On it was a picture of Beth that stared at me where I was sitting, making me feel even more uncomfortable. I was feeling slight symptoms of asthma, but I blamed them on the tense situation. A nervous cramp aggravated my side, my eyes were beginning to itch, and I could feel the formation of a sneeze that would surface at any time.

Finally, Beth barged into the living room with an almost disfigured expression on her face. "I'm sorry I'm so late." She sat down in a stuffed chair beside Mother, and I held my breath. Her hair was disheveled and her hands looked damp, as if they had been washed without a proper drying. I had a strange feeling about what had detained her and a fearful knowledge of what was to come.

"Beth, would you please bring Mrs. Kross a few more mints?" Mrs. Stuckey asked her nicely. Beth didn't refuse the favor; she brought Mother the mints obediently.

"Is that pine soap or perfume that both of you girls are wearing?" Mother asked Beth, as Beth handed her the mints. At that, Mother crossed her legs, catching Beth's glance and her double take. Beth looked at me with questions and answers, and she fell back into her chair with momentary despondency.

"Mrs. Kross, where did you get those unusual shoes?" Beth asked, recovering from her realization.

"Ada gave them to me for Mother's Day. Aren't they nice? It was quite a surprise. I usually have an idea what she's going to buy, but this year she didn't even share her secret with her father."

"They are pretty," Mrs. Stuckey agreed. "Beth gave me this African violet." Mrs. Stuckey pointed to the plant sitting on the table by the window.

I was feeling fainter by the minute from Beth's hateful glances when Beth suddenly said, "If you don't mind, Mother and Mrs. Kross, I would like to shoe—I mean show—Ada my room. She hasn't seen Grandmother's antique locket and I promised her I'd show it to her." Beth stood up and I stood up, too. Our mothers' faces had shown approval.

"Come on, Ada," she dictated to me. By this time I was feeling strong symptoms of asthma, and my side cramp and stomach twists were worsening. My eyes were itching and I felt like I was squinting. My breath was getting less and less easy to catch. Any other time Mother would have noticed, but today she was on a cloud.

Beth led me to her room without a look or a word. Once we stepped in, she closed the door, shut her shutters and slowly turned her stare on me. Her red hair looked pale beside the blush of her skin, and her eyes no longer looked cool. They were sending sparks.

"So! You're the one who's been taking my shoes! What a fake you are. Pretending to help me watch for the thief! If your mother wasn't such a pleasant person, I'd walk back down those stairs and back into the living room and yank my shoes off of her unsuspecting feet. But she's too kind. As outraged as I am, I couldn't tell her that her only daughter is a sneaky, conniving, malicious thief."

My feelings of desperation weren't helped by the suspicion that she was right. "You've got to let me explain; it's not like that. . . ." I sat down on her bed and tried to remain as calm as I could in such a sick state of body and mind. "You see, my mother wears your shoe size, and—"

"I don't want to hear any more alibis. I'm sick of lies." She paced the floor in rage. And I felt I had to fight back in spite of my worsening asthma.

"You're living a lie yourself. If I didn't respect *your* parents, I'd go down those stairs and tell them what their darling daughter is doing," I said.

"You're in too much trouble yourself, Ada."

"I'm only guilty of borrowing those shoes for a Mother's Day present. I was going to pay you for them or replace them myself." It was beginning to be painful for me to talk.

"Hah!" Her body heaved with the weight of her anger. "Like all the others?" She folded her arms and stared daggers into me.

"I didn't take the others." I rubbed my irritated eyes. I was so short of breath that I could hardly take my part without gasping between syllables.

"What's wrong with you, Ada? Your eyes are puffy and you're breathing like you've been running." She forgot the situation for a second.

"I don't know. But like—I was trying—to tell you." I gasped for air. "I forgot—Mother's Day."

At that moment a yellow long-haired cat poked its head out from under the bed and pounced onto my lap, purring loudly and rubbing against my cheek.

"Oh no! It's no wonder I'm so sick. I'm allergic to cats! I could die!"

"Fluff, get down." Beth threw the cat off me and I ran downstairs, blurting the news to my parents in the most undignified manner.

"They have—" I sneezed, "a cat! I'm sorry—" I sneezed again, "but I'm sick."

My parents rushed me home, reassuring the Stuckeys that apologies were not needed. Beth had tears in her eyes when I left, but I was too sick to think about the future of our friendship.

Once I was away from the cat atmosphere, my asthma subsided considerably. Mother gave me a pill and put me to bed to sit under the filtered air of my air conditioner. I had hardly warmed my sheets when I heard a knock at my door and a girl's voice saying my name. At first I thought I was imagining things, but then the voice spoke again.

"Ada, it's Beth. Beth Stuckey."

"Beth, come in." I was beginning to wonder how the day would end.

Beth took one step in and stopped to look at me.

"Come closer," I said. "This isn't a deathbed."

"Your parents said you would be here and they told me to come up and calm you. I know I'm in no position to do that, but I did want to apologize." She looked down at the floor as if she found her courage there. Then she looked at me again. "I believe your story about the shoes. I don't want this misunderstanding to ruin the beginning of what could become a wonderful friendship. Can you ever forgive me?"

"Oh, Beth, it's you that needs to forgive me! I took advantage of your secret. That's the most conniving thing I've ever done to a friend and the most dishonest thing I've ever done to my mother. The money for the shoes I borrowed is in the envelope on my dresser. Take it on your way out. I think it will cover the cost."

"Thank you," Beth said. "It was quite a shoe mix-up, for sure." Then she looked around. "Your room's lovely—like out of a magazine. A picture window and your very own air conditioner too. Could I spend the night some time when it's hot?" She tiptoed around, running her fingers across the furniture wood and picking up what-nots on my shelves.

"I'd love for you to spend the night," I said, anticipating all those hours of talking.

"Let's do it soon!" She sat on my bed with a bounce. Then I lost her as she fell into deep thought.

"Ada, I had the most beautiful dream last night! I dreamed it in color too. It all started when I went to my shoe hideaway and found shoes buried there, a pair for every color in the rainbow." She closed her eyes for a moment, trying to visualize the scene again. "They were the most beautiful shoes I'd ever seen! One pair was the color of rain, clear as glass. Everywhere I stuck my shovel, I struck another shoe box. There was a fortune in shoes!"

"Maybe that dream has a special meaning. Maybe it means that you'll find your shoes again!" I said, daydreaming a little myself.

"That would be a dream come true." She walked over to my dresser and began opening the bottles of perfume my mother had given me and sampling the different scents on her wrist. "Is there anything in this world, Ada, that you love as much as I love shoes?" She turned to my shelf of angels. "What's this?"

"They're angels. I collect them." I held my breath. She was the first person outside of my family who had ever handled them.

"They're positively breathtaking. Do you believe in real angels?"

"Yes." I was waiting for her to laugh.

"Well, I'm religious. I tithe a nickel a week of my allowance and I have a black velvet kneeling pillow in my bedroom. I pray nightly. You haven't seen an angel, have you?"

"Not exactly. But I want to." It would have been easy for me, then, to betray Mr. Pearl's confidence and tell her about his angel, but I stopped myself. She seemed sincere, if not devout, as she cautiously turned my statues over in her hand and commented on them. Still, only time would prove her to be a trusted friend.

"I like this one especially. There's a little figurine that looks like it in the drugstore in town. I was going to buy it for my room, but since my shoe robbery I haven't got a dime to spare." Her enthusiasm lessened as she remembered her predicament.

"I have an idea that might help you, Beth," I said, although I knew Father would probably disown me for hiring more help for him. "Dad will have green beans ready to pick this Saturday. If you want to help pick them, I'm sure he'll pay you a fair wage."

"Would he?" She looked hopeful.

"Yes, and of course you'll meet the other fieldhands. You've already met Burl."

"Is that Wiggins with a *W*?" She tried to remember it.

"No. It's Higgins with an *H*, as in 'hellion.' " I snickered. "He's a loner. His family is dead and no one says why. And then there's Mr. Pearl. You'll want to hug him; he's as soft as pillow stuffing. And Freddie, he's our age. He has never seen the actual light of day. He has an eyesight problem, but his biggest problem is his weight. He's as fat as a prized pig. Of course there are more fieldhands than that. You'll meet them all."

"That would be wonderful. I need to buy so many things. My supply of nylon hose is getting low. This pair is practically gone." She pulled up her skirt a few inches higher, revealing a hole the size of her knee. "But no one's the wiser as long as my skirt stays in place," she said with a sly look on her face as she let the skirt fall below her knee again.

"Those nylons do fit your legs perfectly." I was sick with envy.

"Yes, they do. I buy them at Krums. I always have and I always will," she said with authority as she examined her stockings for more holes.

"Is that a secret from your parents, too?" I was waiting to hear her technique for that.

"No. They agreed to let me wear nylons at the beginning of the year. Seventh grade is a good time to start but at my old school a lot of girls begin wearing them in the fifth or sixth grade, when they start wearing makeup."

"And you shave your legs, too, don't you?"

"Yes. Don't you?" I was grateful that I was bedridden at that moment.

"I don't do anything! At Mount Mercer there isn't one interesting soul that I care to impress." I was ashamed of the truth, but I told it. "Do you have a boyfriend?" I asked.

"Not exactly—it's really one-sided. I'm still considered a new girl." Beth sat down on the carpeting and looked out of the window. "Steve Sasser!" She whispered the words as if she worshiped the very sound of them. "He rides the school bus and has the straightest teeth I've ever seen. . . . I'm getting braces myself this fall. I hope they will help my teeth and my lisp."

"It's hardly noticeable," I said.

"I know, but sometimes when I get extremely nervous or excited I talk too fast and saliva escapes. Once I had to ask Mr. Barbel a question in class, and when I got close enough to him for him to hear me, I—well I spit in his eye." Beth blushed from the memory. "I don't have to tell you that I roasted from embarrassment."

"Don't worry, Beth. The braces will help. I'm not so sure what will help me. See?" I smiled my toothiest to show the space between my two front teeth. "Maybe I need braces, too. But my parents think this gap is cute."

"Oh, I'm sure they would be kind enough to take you to a dentist for braces if you asked them," Beth said comfortingly, then changed the subject again. "Do you mind if I look in your closet?"

"Of course not. It's over there."

Beth trotted across the room and opened the closet door. I knew she would be impressed with the beautiful dresses mother had sewn for me. Many of the dresses I had never worn, although they were copies of those seen in the latest fashion magazines.

"I can't believe your wardrobe," she said after a few minutes.

"And your shoes—they're simply gorgeous!" She raved and used a different word of flattery for every pair she uncovered in my closet. "I wouldn't be ashamed to be seen in any of these. What size do you wear?"

"Size five. My feet are awfully small."

"There's nothing awful about that. It's too bad we don't wear the same shoe size. We could swap now and then. I wonder if my type of corrective shoe could help your pigeon toes?" She wasn't really asking, just thinking out loud. "Isn't our situation exasperating? You've got the shoes, but you can't show the legs you've got. I can show my legs, but I don't have the shoes!" She shook her head as she straightened the boxes again.

"Don't give up, Beth. Things might work out for us. And as for your lost shoes, well, you'll just have to start saving for a new supply."

"I've got to have a new pair to wear on the last day of school. These are from gym class." She stared disapprovingly at the sneakers on her feet. "Don't ever mention my wearing them." She winked, and I understood perfectly. Then she went on, "On the last day of school, almost all the girls dress up in their very best. It's a tradition. Maybe the money you paid me and the money I make working for your father will be enough to buy a really nice pair. If your father really will be so kind as to hire me."

"You'll get the job." I stood up and brushed my hair with unusual care as I talked to Beth through the mirror. "You know there's only one good thing about Mount Mercer Private School. We get out two weeks earlier than the public schools. We're out for the summer in ten days."

"How lucky for you. Why don't you come to Eagle Creek with me on the last day of school? We're allowed to have guests. It's only a month away, and you can dress up, too. Would you want that? Please say that you will."

"I don't think so, Beth. But thanks anyway." I knew it was out of the question.

"Why in the world did you enroll in a place like Mount Mercer? I heard it was incredibly dull and childish."

"Because of this." I pulled one of my asthma masks out of a drawer. Beth looked at it like it was a snakeskin. I wasn't expecting such a severe reaction; she seemed so levelheaded. But I knew she was having flashbacks of the morning through the mist.

"Wh-what is that?"

"It's my asthma mask. Do you remember seeing it before?" I held it over my face to give the full effect of it, then I took it off again, feeling embarrassed for ever showing it. "I didn't mean to frighten you that morning."

"Ada, I don't know what to say."

"I'd be the target for every joke. I wanted a backwoods school. Can you blame me?"

"I'm sorry for my nosiness." Beth carefully turned and closed my closet door, then faced me again, regaining her composure. "You don't have to wear your asthma mask all the time, do you?"

"Not unless the pollen count is high, but in the fall and spring that can be all the time."

"Then I think you *should* come with me to Eagle Creek on the last day of school. It's quite necessary for your self-confidence. I'm positive that the kids worth knowing wouldn't laugh once they got to know you. I'm not laughing. I'm just a little shocked because I've never seen a mask like that before. Promise me you'll consider it."

"All right, I'll consider it. But that's all."

Mother called us down for a snack, and Beth fit in with my family like a lost child finally home. She chatted with Mother and asked Father so many questions about the garden. Of course, he felt flattered and answered every one. He even suggested that she come and pick green beans and strawberries with me, if we promised to work and not visit. We promised, and then Beth left long after dark, filled with hope and newly found friendship. I was happier than I had been since I don't know when.

CHAPTER 10

MONDAY AFTER SCHOOL I found Mr. Pearl working in the stake-tomato patch. I followed him up and down the rows as he tied and wrapped every plant.

"Can you imagine having a friend with the name Elizabeth Hathaway Stuckey? She plays the piano. Did I tell you?"

"Yep. You did."

"She plays the piano really well, if you like classical music. Do you like classical music, Mr. Pearl?"

"I like the birds and the music the wind makes. You know I'm simple-minded, Ada. Then there's the silent music that comes time and again."

Silent music was music seldom heard by human ears. According to Mr. Pearl flowers bloomed from it, and insects danced to its tune. There was a natural order about the garden—the insects about their business, the bees spreading pollen with a concentrated hum, the morning glories growing on the grassy edges, and the spiders spinning webs between the leaves.

"Beth said she's found a boyfriend, but she's more like a secret admirer of him. I promised not to tell, but I know I can trust you."

"Don't tell me if she don't want you to."

"It's OK. His name is Steve Sasser. He has her heart beating at his feet. She's in terrible shape and she hardly knows him."

"Love will do that." Mr. Pearl worked his way down the row whistling softly.

"Mr. Pearl, how do you—did you—love Sweet Cindy?" I had never really understood the degrees of feelings that made people caress and cling to one another until their deaths.

"Love just moves inside people and it changes their heart before they can do a thing about it. And when your heart is touched by love, all of a sudden your senses come alive and it's spring. Loves changes your heart the way a rosebud changes into the most beautiful flower you've ever seen."

"I could live without ever seeing a rose. I could."

"But you wouldn't want to live without colors and tasting and smelling. Without love, life is just like looking at a black and white picture."

"Is that what life looks like to you since Sweet Cindy died?"

"Nope. I love her still."

"But she's not here to love you back. It must be lonely, putting all your love into something that can't ever love you back."

"Ada, someday a good man will come along and he'll fill your life so full of love that even if he has to leave you, you'll have had more than your share. That kind of love is stronger than death."

"I don't want a man to fill my life full of love or anything. I don't want to fall in love."

"You will," he said.

"I won't, Mr. Pearl. I know I don't want anything to change my healthy heart."

"Hearts ain't healthy without love." Mr. Pearl hummed. "You silly girl. Don't say you won't, 'cause sure as twice two is four you will, 'cause you said you won't." Mr. Pearl pretended to whittle the dull end of a loose stake, but he was deeper into whittling me!

"Then I'll say now that I *will* fall in love—because that way I *won't*." I stomped my foot at him.

"But then again, Ada, what you confess with your tongue, so be it come to pass, and Ada, you just confessed with your tongue that you will. So you will." He chuckled. "You can't get out of it."

"Then I'll never talk about it again!" I clomped out of the tomato patch, trying not to listen to the soothing tune of Mr. Pearl's whistling.

CHAPTER 11

SATURDAY FINALLY CAME. I was awake at dawn, anticipating Beth's walk through the pine row. She came to work at eight, walking through the blue faces of morning-glory blooms, taking deep breaths of the lingering mist and shouting my name with such familiarity as she waved.

"Ada! Ada!" It seemed that we had always been friends, and perhaps we *had* been since time itself began; it was a mystery I wanted to believe in.

"Beth, hello!" I said. She was not dressed sensibly, but wore white jeans, a white blouse, and white tennis shoes.

"Beth, you look so—so *white*," I stuttered, not wanting to lessen her enthusiasm.

"I know. And when I'm in the sun my skin turns beet-red and then back to paste again."

"No. I'm talking about your clothes. You'll ruin them out here."

"Oh." She studied her attire. "I haven't any work clothes. Not that I can think of."

"What do you do with your old clothes?" I asked. "Your clothes do get old, don't they?"

"Mother puts all my old things in sacks for the missionaries. Maybe I can get something out of those sacks during lunch hour. I'll look."

Father motioned for us and we ran to the bean patch. Beth was eager to begin her task and earn her hourly wage. I knew that visions of lovely new shoes would keep her from tiring too quickly. She was so determined.

"These are the green-bean bushes, and these are green beans." Father picked one from the vine. "The beans should be about this long or they won't be ready to eat."

"Yes. Yes. I see." Beth leaned over and investigated the bush beside her, proudly pulling a green bean from the vine. And she continued to treat each green bean with personal interest, as if each plant had borne separate gifts to please. Of course, she exhausted herself after so many rows, and at one point we lay flat between the bean rows and stared into crystal blue space.

"Lazy little pigs." Freddie had finally made himself known. He had arrived to work late and unfortunately been assigned to the same bean patch. "I've never seen girls so dirty."

It was true that after twenty minutes of scooting along the bean rows and staring into eternity on our backs, we were dust-stricken and looked like we had purposely rolled in the dirt, but Beth's strawberry hair looked immaculate. It was French-braided to perfection.

Freddie stood beside us, appraising Beth with his fuzzy vision and grunting hog-style until I felt pressured to introduce him.

"Beth, this is Freddie Moulton," I said, half-embarrassed. Freddie nodded and shuffled his feet.

"Hello, Fred," Beth said. I had to laugh, which Freddie defensively interpreted to be an insult.

"What's so funny, Ada? You skinny ugly little runt." He turned to Beth. "Call me Fred if you want to." Then he moved importantly on.

"He's flirting with you," I whispered, trying to ease some of the tension.

"I wish Steve Sasser would flirt with my dirt." Beth sighed, shading her eyes from the sun as she looked at me. "Steve Sasser wouldn't notice me if I were tarred and feathered."

"Does he ever speak to you?" I asked her.

"To tell you the tormenting truth, Ada, I don't know. I'm, well, I'm too shy to say anything to him."

"How are you ever going to meet him if you don't speak up? I've not had much experience with boys, but I know you've got to have enough guts to say hello and look them eye to eye."

"Not his eyes, Ada." Beth's dazed eyes grew tearful as she discussed him. "Steve has the bluest eyes I've ever seen. Like eyes out of a priceless painting. His eyes make me want to weep."

"Who has the bluest eyes?" Freddie moved closer to where Beth and I were supposedly working.

"No one said a word about eyes," I tried to cover for her. "Beth said she—she hasn't seen such blue skies."

"Oh." Freddie moved down the row a bit further.

"Hasn't Steve ever said anything to you?" I whispered.

"Once . . . he stepped on my shoe, one of the lost brown ones with the brass buckles. He looked up at me, smiled like a movie star, and said, 'Excuse me.' I actually felt dizzy and I turned pink." She was blushing then just from talking about him. "It's more than infatuation. Just the sound of the name, Steve Sasser, saps my strength."

"Then don't say it again," I said. "We'll never get the green beans picked." It was frightening to think that the mere mention of a person's name could change one's whole metabolism.

"Did someone say Steve Sasser's name? He's my second cousin." Freddie scooted closer again. He pointed to Beth's guilty face. "It was you! I bet you're in love with him. You're in love with my cousin!"

"No! No!" Beth's face flushed wildly. "I said . . .uh, 'Spring is finally here and I sure did miss her.' " Beth looked tragically at me before hiding her face in the nearest bean bush.

"Phooey! You love my cousin. You love Stevie. Stevie. Stevie." Beth batted her eyes in a panic.

"Stop bothering Beth," I said. "Don't you dare tell Steve a lie like that."

"Don't worry. He doesn't speak to me." Freddie's words were pitifully honest, but his voice was light. "He's too popular. He's captain of the baseball team in the spring and the football team in the fall. He's on the track team too. I call him Pretty Boy Sasser. I don't care if he doesn't speak to me. I don't need him. I don't need any friends," Freddie said matter-of-factly. "I don't need anybody. I'm saving my money to join the foreign legion. They take anybody, and I can go there and be a hero like my father."

Freddie pulled out his father's war medal for Beth, proudly exhibiting each side of it on his plump padded palm. It was then that I turned to continue my work and noticed Burl and Hank standing like two scarecrows at the end of the bean patch. They swayed at the hips with their hands in their pockets, their mouths moving with sly twists as they carried on a private conversation. Hank spoke out first.

"Hey, Hippo," Hank said. Laughter. Insults. Freddie's ears reddened. A flush started in the fatty creases of his neck and traveled up his face. He didn't acknowledge Hank. Instead, he turned his attention to the green-bean bushes, picking as fast as his plump fingers could snap them from the vine.

"Hippo." This time the intruder's voice was Burl's.

Freddie stared into the bean bush, not volunteering a word. Then he puffed up and blew out his words, much like a big balloon losing all its air.

"Smelly, sweaty, rotten animals on two feet," he said under his breath. He continued to pick green beans, obviously wishing he could disappear.

"Hippo, come here." Burl graveled his voice. "You deaf and blind?"

Freddie puffed up again. "Stupid, ugly, dirty, no good, stinking." He directed his words to the ground, the sweat dripping off of his forehead.

"I guess we'll just have to go after him," Hank said out loud. "This is your last chance, Hippo."

Freddie quietly cursed, his muscles resisting with hatred and hostility. Then he stood up, beaten, and began his walk toward Burl, who seemed to have invisible reins on him.

"That's more like it." Burl sounded pleased.

"Hank and me got something for you," Burl said after Freddie stopped in front of him. Hank pulled a green tomato out of his pocket. "We brought you a nice, juicy apple."

"That's no apple," Freddie whined. "That's a tomato that ain't ripe yet."

Burl looked at Hank with adult aggravation. "Hank, this boy thinks we don't know the difference between a tomato and an apple."

"What are we going to do about it?" Hank asked Burl.

Burl studied Freddie for a strenuous moment. "Eat it!" he demanded.

Freddie looked at Hank, who held the green tomato. Then Burl took a step closer. Freddie quickly took the tomato from Hank and took an obedient bite.

"Oh yeck! It's too sour." He leaned over, spit out the bits of tomato, and gagged until I thought his quivering insides would explode with revulsion.

"Hippo, you ain't worth two cents." Burl displayed a superior disgust. "But for two cents you can lick the dirt off my boots. Now be a good boy and do it for a good beating."

"Do what?" For a moment Freddie could not comprehend Burl's cruelty.

"You heard me, lick my boot."

Finally Freddie realized that Burl meant business, and he slowly submitted into a kneeling position.

"Don't do it, Freddie," I shouted. "I'd rather die twice than kiss Burl's feet." Freddie looked at me lamely and I could feel his misery.

"Shut up, Ugly, unless you want to see Hippo crawl, too," Burl said to me victoriously.

"You're the snake," I shouted. "Let's see you crawl."

Burl planted his hand firmly on the back of Freddie's neck and began to force Freddie's face down to boot level. Mr. Pearl must have sensed the trouble. He ran to where Burl stood, pulled Freddie to his feet, and got between the two boys.

"Burl, you got no business over here. Get back where you

belong." Mr. Pearl took control of the situation with a firm grip on Burl's shoulder, giving Burl a push in the direction of the melon patch. Burl moved sluggishly on, but there was friction when their eyes met.

When Beth saw Mr. Pearl, a strange twinkle came into her eyes. She must have seen beyond the whiskers, wrinkles, and faded clothes into the finer delicacies confined to his interior.

"Who is that man?" she asked after Mr. Pearl had disappeared into the pin oaks.

"Mr. Pearl. Remember, I told you about him. He's my very best friend."

"Where did he come from?" she asked. "And when can I meet him?"

"Yoo hoo. Yoo hoo. Is anybody in there?" It was Beth's voice coming from the other side of the pin oak's leaves and branches. Tippy Ten perked up his ears and thumped his tail on the damp earth. He must have sensed her friendliness.

"Beth, everybody's in here," I said. "Come on in."

Beth maneuvered her way in with some difficulty. She had hurried home at noon to change into blue jeans rolled to her knees and a faded green shirt. She wore sneakers—a different style and color on each foot. Her little toe stuck through a hole in one sneaker, but her toenail was painted with bright polish.

"Now you look like one of us," I said to Beth, who wasn't listening, but absorbing the beauty of her surroundings: the specks of sky through a hundred layers of interlocking leaves.

"This is absolutely heavenly," she sighed. "I feel like I'm in a cathedral."

"We love it," I said with omnipotent pride.

"I've never seen such a place," she continued. "It's like a secret room. No one would ever know you were here if they walked by. And it's cool. The sun never touches you."

Finally Beth's gaze rested upon Mr. Pearl. He smiled; the natural resources of one gentle look made the moment magical.

"Beth, I want you to meet Mr. Pearl." I introduced the precious old to the wonderful new.

"How do you do?" Beth said. Mr. Pearl tipped his hat. Beth shook his hand and made herself a friend.

Then Mr. Pearl arranged a special seat for Beth out of fallen branches. After she was situated comfortably, he settled beside Freddie, who was still fighting back tears of humiliation and fear.

"Ada and me eat our lunch here 'bout every day," Mr. Pearl said. "Freddie too, since he started working here. I got some extra peanut-butter sandwiches in my lunch bucket for anybody who's hungry."

"I wouldn't mind a bit." Beth used her best etiquette as she delicately handled her sandwich half. Tippy Ten sat close by at attention, his two white paws together, his long mouth salivating.

"I'm going to quit." Freddie hid his miserable face in his pudgy hands and trembled. For once I could understand his cowardly ways.

"Perk up, Freddie. You're going to do just fine." Mr. Pearl put his hand on Freddie's shoulder, and the reassuring touch seemed to help. "I know you're suffering, but suffering can make you stronger, ever braver. That's part of becoming a man. Learning how to suffer and understanding when it can and can't be changed. It ain't a sin to suffer when it ain't your own fault, but if you're suffering because you're a coward, then it's a sin and a shame."

"You're saying that sweating from working hard on the garden in the sun isn't a bad kind of suffering, but running from Burl is." Freddie brushed a stray tear away with his arm by pretending to wipe the sweat off his forehead. "But it's not right for me to get picked on by boys like them."

"I told you Burl would start trouble," I said to Mr. Pearl, "and I don't see him suffering one bit."

"There are thousands of Burls in this world, Ada." Mr. Pearl's delivery was quick. "You can't run away from all of them"

"A girl wanted to beat me up," Beth said. She had been listening thoughtfully in the shadows of the leaves. "It was my first week of Eagle Creek, too. I was just as frightened as you, Freddie."

"You?" Freddie looked at her oddly. "What did you do to deserve it?"

"Nothing," Beth shrugged her shoulders. "The girl said I spat on her."

"What does spat mean?" Freddie asked.

"Spit. You know, spit," I said.

"Did you spit on her?" Freddie laughed his ornery laugh.

"Certainly not. I mean, it wasn't deliberate. It was my lisp that caused my saliva to fly."

"Did you fight her?" Freddie asked, somewhat encouraged by the incident.

"Of course not. It's animalistic for girls to fight with their fists," Beth said quite properly.

"I'd like to knock Hank and Burl's heads together. Pow! Pow!" Freddie laughed with delight.

"Hank is nothing but a baby sheep when it comes to following in Burl's tracks," I said. "Mr. Pearl, how can Freddie fight them?"

"Show me," Freddie said. "My mother doesn't believe in fighting. She's scared of a ladybug."

"Stand up, Freddie," Mr. Pearl appraised the problem. "Look tough. Look mean. Look strong. Look powerful!" Freddie's fat cheeks and chin hung down like a bloodhound's. All of his expressions looked the same.

"I know. It's hopeless," Freddie groaned. Beth and I secretly agreed. "I couldn't scare a cross-eyed kitten," he said.

Mr. Pearl took off his weathered hat and adjusted it. "Looking mean isn't everything, Freddie," Mr. Pearl said. "Another thing to do when a bully threatens you is to take a deeeeep breath and smile."

"Smile?" Freddie looked more discouraged than ever. "Can you just see me smiling at Burl?" Freddie smiled his silliest.

"Then look him in the eye and say, 'My oh my,' even if you'd rather run a mile."

"What if he calls me a name?" Freddie asked. "Like fatso or hippo?"

"Stand tall and lean forward, sayin', 'Oh is that so?' " Mr. Pearl demonstrated with all the enthusiasm he could muster.

"What if he says, 'Yes, it is so'?"

"Then you say, 'No.' But be cool and polite when a bully wants to fight." Mr. Pearl's eyes began to twinkle and his foot started tapping as he continued. "Excuse him when he swings his fist and thank him when he misses . . . " He paused in thought for a second before continuing triumphantly, "Apologize when you black his eyes, but forget the get-well kisses."

"Incredible!" cried Beth. "It's a poem. Do some more!"

Mr. Pearl was enjoying himself. "Hem and haw before you kick and claw. Snarl and spit before you bite or hit! Make him move fast so his energy won't last. And when he's moving slow . . . let the punches go!" Mr. Pearl finished with a tip of his hat and a deep blow.

"More. More. More." Freddie and Beth were bouncing up and down where they sat.

With that, Mr. Pearl whistled a knee-slapping tune and I watched Beth's and Freddie's faces, which were more entertaining than the songs. Beth got to her feet and tap-danced in the dust until we all spilled over with laughter and relief.

Something happened that day in the pin oaks. Mr. Pearl, who had always looked immortal to me, now looked as if he might perish after all. The colors of his eyes, hair, and skin seemed to be wearing thin. Solid as he was, his strength was less of skin and bone and more of spirit. When he recited the bully poem, he looked ghostly enough to float through the foliage. He seemed so close to dust and ashes, almost too fragile to touch. The spring was taking its toll on all of us.

THAT AFTERNOON Beth taught me to French-braid my hair. Then she manicured my nails a frightful red, so startling that Puddin refused to sit on my hand.

"Hank and Burl are too cruel to be true. Poor Freddie," she

said as she witnessed the first plucking of my eyebrows. "Just imagine. Freddie is a relative of Steve Sasser!"

"Oh no! This hurts! I'd rather be ugly!" I shuddered with each yank of the tweezers. "This is what I call cruelty!"

"Do you mean you'd rather be a bushy-browed bore?" Beth turned up her petite nose at the thought of it. "Ada, if you could only see the difference. Your eyes are the biggest, saddest eyes in this hemisphere."

"Sad is right! My eyebrows are nothing but swollen sores," I squinted into the mirror. "Do I have to do this? Am I so ugly that we can't overlook it?"

"Ada, look at your eyebrows. One is plucked and one is un-plucked. Now *that* is ugly!"

I groaned at my dilemma, then plucked away, feeling like a human chicken.

"You do want to look beautiful when you go with me to Eagle Creek, don't you? You have great potential, Ada."

"For pain? I know that." Just then I wished that she were Mr. Pearl, who loved me for my simple self. No chance.

"Don't worry about your eyebrows. The swelling will go down," Beth laughed. "Your eyes are so warm they could melt a . . . a . . . "

I knew she would think of an appropriate description. She was capable of describing anything, from a "perfect pouting" green pea to a "delicately detailed" dewdrop.

"Popsicle! That's it. Your eyes are that warm. You'll be a knock-out when you finish."

Then Beth pulled a razor from her purse. The blade in it looked sharp enought to skin a cat. She casually handed me the razor. I took a bar of soap with the other hand.

"Don't be nervous, Ada," she said. My hands were shaking noticeably as I covered my legs with a soapy lather. "No one has ever died from shaving their legs yet. Don't think about it. Just do it mechanically. Watch it, Ada! Watch it!"

The instant the steel edge touched my skin, it drew blood. I applied a piece of tissue to my skin and left it on the violated spot, hoping my blood would clot. Then I continued on due course from my ankles to my knees, all the while wishing I had a steadier hand. Every few inches I would nick my skin again and more blood would run until I thought I would not live to see the end of it. At one point I became dizzy and had to stop and put my head between my knees. All the while Beth encouraged me.

"With those smooth legs you'll look as graceful as a swan," she said when the bleeding had finally stopped and I had washed the bloody streaks away.

"Will I need a blood transfusion every time I shave them?" I asked with a scowl, although I was thrilled with the results.

"You'll become an expert in no time," Beth said.

With that, Beth returned her coveted razor to her purse. Before my legs were hardly dry, she was holding a tube of lipstick out to me, saying, "Pucker up, Ada."

"Pucker up, how?"

"Like this." She demonstrated, then stopped to watch my attempt. She took the tube from me and I watched while she strategically applied the lipstick over her moving mouth.

"You know, Ada, I've never been kissed." It was something I would never have admitted.

"Do you want to be kissed?" I asked.

"Yes. I do. But I want to be kissed by someone special. I want a solid kisser, not some ridiculous boy with bologna on his breath."

"Have you ever been kissed, Ada?" she asked.

"That stupid Freddie tried." At this, we broke into a torrent of laughter, falling to the floor and rolling from side to side.

"Oh, Ada! What did you do?" Beth nearly ruptured her appendix.

"I slapped him in the face!" I said. It was the first time I had had the confidence to laugh about it.

"Just like they did in the old movies!" Beth laughed until she cried. Then she sat up dreamy-eyed. "I would love, simply love, Steve Sasser to kiss me to soft music and candlelight." She stood up and began waltzing around the room, pretending to be dancing with him. "Steve would look at me and say, 'Elizabeth, you are so light on your feet. May I kiss you tonight?' " She screamed with delight, then fell back into a trance-like state. "Then I would say,

'That would be lovely, Steven.' Or maybe, 'If you wish.' Then we would twirl until we were both dizzy. You know—the same effect adults get from expensive champagne. And he would pull me close to him until I could hardly breathe." Beth stopped and caught her breath.

"And then you'd close your eyes!" I finished for her.

"No. I'd want to see every minute of it. Oh, Ada." She sighed, and I worried that she would spend the next hour in a swooning session.

"What if Burl kissed you instead?" I said, knowing that the mention of his name would snap her out of it.

"Burl?" Beth rolled her eyes. "What would *you* do?"

"I'd get leprosy for sure. My lips would probably curdle," I said. Beth and I whooped again.

"I can see it all now." Beth made her voice as sinister as she could. "Burl pulls you into a dark corner."

"Beth, stop it! Your imagination has gone wild. He's a monster. If his looks can kill, his kisses probably paralyze. Burl likes the kind of women who pose in magazines. The sheriff said Burl's car was full of them."

"Of women?" Beth's eyes widened.

"No. Of magazines."

"The women in those magazines have figures most men look at," Beth said as she appraised her posture in the mirror and then made a dissatisfied face. "I'm sure Steve Sasser would look at them."

"It's hopeless for me," I said. I was certain I would always be as thin as onion skin.

"No, Ada," Beth said. She made circles with her arms and I knew she was far from finished with my beauty regimen. "It helps your chest muscles."

"Really?"

"Yes. My chest muscles develop daily. So will yours. If you *don't* do this, you will be as flat as the floor."

"My muscles are already sore. Why do you want to make it worse?"

"Beauty is work. It is a fact of life. Ask any beautiful woman and she'll tell you it doesn't come naturally. Now, up with your arms." I circled them.

"Put this book on your head and walk with it." I did it obediently.

"Does loving Steve Sasser make you happy?" I asked her.

"Oh, he makes me so happy and sad, I don't know which is which." She picked up the book and tried to balance it. "You'll see him for yourself, when you come with me to Eagle Creek on the last day of school."

"LOOK AT ME," I said to Mr. Pearl when he stopped in the barn to stack baskets before quitting time.

"What am I supposed to see?" Mr. Pearl studied me.

"Do I look different? Better?" No one seemed to notice the results of my painful improvement—except negatively.

"You look pretty, but I don't know what is so different about that."

"It's hopeless," I said. "I want to know if my eyes look larger."

"Well, I guess so. It's your eyebrows. You drew lines on them."

"Beth helped me. She's a whiz with eyes and shoes."

Mr. Pearl stroked his whiskers and chuckled through their stiffness. "I wonder where Beth learned to toe-tap like that."

"Knowing Beth, it probably just came natural," I said. Then I thought of something else. "Are you going to teach Freddie to fight?"

"I suppose, with what energy I got left in me."

"Mr. Pearl, how can you tell if a bird is a girl or a boy?" Surely he could teach me something new, too. I enjoyed sharing him, but I sometimes missed our solitude.

"You know by the colors of the feathers on most birds. The males are always prettier than the females. The females' feathers are dull."

"All pigeons look the same to me. What do you think Puddin is?"

"Well, if Puddin lays an egg, we'll know he's a she. I don't know, Ada. Don't matter to me."

"Don't matter to me either, except I was curious as to what to call Puddin instead of 'it.' 'It' is kind of insulting."

"Just call the bird Puddin and let 'it' be," he chuckled.

"I guess. I think it's time to teach this bird a new trick." I called Tippy Ten over. He was napping in a large sunbeam but was quick to oblige. He soon stood at my side, unaware of my motive.

"Stay, Tippy." I gently placed Puddin on Tippy Ten's back.

"Ada, that dog might swallow that bird up!" Mr. Pearl was nonetheless amused.

"He knows better. Good dog." The hair on Tippy Ten's back stood on end. Puddin protested at first by flapping its wings and squawking. When Tippy Ten remained unmoved, the pigeon finally relaxed.

"If that ain't something." Mr. Pearl walked closer to where we were standing. "I ought to have a picture of that."

Tippy Ten sensed some sympathy in Mr. Pearl and moved toward him. Puddin managed to stay on his back for a few steps, but then panicked and fell off. In the process of the fall, it flapped its wings.

"I believe that bird might fly if you gave it a reason." Mr. Pearl put the top of his hand under the bird's claws and the bird stepped onto it. Tippy sniffed the ground where the bird had first landed.

"I don't think he's really healed enough for flying yet," I said. I had watched Puddin's wing carefully—as feathers grew in to replace those that had been broken and taped.

"You ever tried to make him fly? You've seen how mother birds push their babies out of the nest," Mr. Pearl said.

"Don't try it!" I quickly took Puddin off his hand and onto mine. "Those babies' wings were in working order. Puddin's wing has been broken. Who's to say it will ever be the same?"

"Ada, you got to give that bird a chance. It can't live its life in a melon crate with its foot tied to a piece of twine."

"Stop bossin' me. It's my bird. I'll let it go when it's good and ready."

"You mean, when *you're* good and ready." Mr. Pearl said. Sometimes he was closer to me than my conscience.

"Mr. Pearl, do you think growing and changing is such a good thing?" I asked him.

"Things got to change. People got to grow. Sometimes it hurts, but that's part of life."

"I suppose. Mother is putting herself through changes by having that baby. I don't know why. We don't need it. Things are fine just the way they are."

The baby was growing daily, making Mother's movements a little more cautious and her body heavy. It was the first time she had ever appeared awkward. Still, her beauty thrived.

"Ada, you need that brother or sister." Mr. Pearl's face was as good as a scolding.

"For what?" What made me fear the unknown? Something as innocent as a baby. Still, I was afraid to consent to it.

"Life goes on, and the baby will help to make the future. Besides, you said the same kinds of things before you met Beth. Remember?"

"That's true," I said. But I was still determined to protest. "I don't want it. Maybe the baby won't fit in with the rest of us."

"You'll love it sure as you're sittin' here," Mr. Pearl said. The wind moved through the old barn's cracks, and the light of the setting sun fell on Mr. Pearl's feet. His old work shoe dulled the shine.

I KNEW IT WAS SELFISH to keep Puddin confined. I wanted to keep it regardless, with its gentle beak, its small intuitive eyes that shone. Its soft dowdy feathers were like delicate velvet.

"Come on, Puddin. It's time for you to fly." I had secretly gone to the barn after quitting time and coaxed the pigeon out of the crate, still tied to the twine.

Puddin strutted from my fingers to my palm, not suspecting that I would boost it into the air. When I did, the pigeon panicked but spread its injured wing naturally and glided onto the barn floor. After it landed safely, it looked up at me and squawked.

"Oh, stop your scolding." I wiped a tear from my eye. "You're not quite flying, but you're getting better."

After three more attempts, Puddin was able to move its wings more rapidly, but each time, after gliding to the floor, it looked up at me with uncertainty.

I picked up the bird. It was warm and plump in my palm.

"Do you want to be free?" I said. "Maybe tomorrow." The bird nodded its little head.

CHAPTER 12

My FINAL DAY AT MOUNT MERCER Private School came at last. It was wonderful to feel free, with the entire summer spread out before me like a cool green bed of grass. I had anticipated a light-hearted day of parting, but Freddie managed to make my last morning at school miserable by calling me a "painted tainted doll" and drawing attention to my eyebrows and lipstick.

"Ada's mouth is bleeding," he shouted, making me want to die a hundred deaths. "Ada's legs look like she's been snakebit."

"And to think I pitied you because of Burl!" I shouted. I hated my vulnerability.

By early afternoon, school had been dismissed for the summer and I was daydreaming about a new life at Eagle Creek. Freddie worked that afternoon, but I was too annoyed to join him.

"I'll go anywhere to school next year, but not Mount Mercer. Freddie is driving me crazy," I said to Mother.

"Mrs. Moulton said that Freddie has saved twenty-five dollars, lost twelve pounds, and marches constantly," Mother said while I had a sandwich. "I wonder why he marches."

"He thinks he's going to join the foreign legion and be a hero like his father," I told her. Freddie had a dream and I spoke of it too lightly. "But don't tell Mrs. Moulton or she'll have an attack."

"I won't say a word about it." Mother stood beside the stove

100

and stared at me. "Ada, you look different. What have you done to your face?" She smiled radiantly, making me feel plain and foolish for trying. "Are you wearing some kind of makeup? I don't mind as long as it isn't too showy. No red lipstick."

"Beth gave me some free samples from the five and ten. She gave me some rouge. That's why it looks like I'm blushing."

"You look fifteen years old. You're growing up too fast."

She rubbed her rounded stomach unconsciously.

"I don't feel fifteen. I'm still the same. How do you think the baby is?" I tried to sound concerned about it, but I was really concerned about my mother. To me, the baby was still an unidentified object.

"Fine. The doctor listened to its heartbeat yesterday."

"Do you mean it has a heartbeat already?" Sometimes life amazed me.

"Oh, yes. It's quite alive. And the baby moves. Her eyes searched mine seeking my approval of the facts of life. "It moves more and more every day."

There was a knock at the back door. It was Rexy.

"There's trouble out there," she said. She pointed to where Burl and Leonard were rocking the outhouse from side to side.

"Help! Help!" It was a muffled cry.

"Did you hear that?" Mother and I rushed outside.

"It's Freddie again." I ran to his rescue. "Burl, stop that! I'm calling my father."

"We ain't doin' a thing," Burl said. He stopped rocking the outhouse. "Come on out, Hippo."

"Yip. Yip. Yip." Hank had to be part beast.

"I can't come out and you know it." Freddie actually sounded angry.

"Freddie, come out here," I said.

"Burl stole my pants." I heard Freddie whimpering through the wooden walls. Hank guffawed and grinned at me. "I told him I'd buy the da-dern things. Me and Burl were goin' to make a tent out of 'em."

"Very funny," I said. "We could all laugh at you, too, but instead it's just plain pity."

"Ada, you're so knock-kneed, I can hear you coming a mile away. Now that's what I call a pity. You tryin' to act grown up."

"Oh, help, help, help!" Freddie was fading fast.

"I wish you'd get out of this town. You're about as funny as a funeral," I said. "You don't have any right to look at my legs. You're supposed to keep your eyes on your work. But that's impossible, isn't it, because you're so lazy."

"What's the matter, Ada? Don't you want boys to look at you? Ain't that why you painted your face and cut up your legs?" Burl knew he had scored. I could feel my face on fire.

"I don't even consider you a boy. You're a low-class untouchable." I spat out the words. Burl's face remained callous, but his eyes looked wounded for an instant.

"Well, you ain't an untouchable." Burl straightened his shoulders and took an intimidating step toward me. I broke out into a sweat when he stood too close. He was evil. There was something untamed about him, like a wild animal pretending to be domestic.

"Somebody help me! There's a wasp in here," Freddie screamed. "Ada, whose side are you on? Help me before I dieeee."

I had hoped he would suffocate from the outhouse's smell of distinction. I was sick of both of them. I ran for Father, who made Burl recover Freddie's pants.

"My medal's gone!" Freddie turned his pockets inside out as he walked out of the outhouse. "My father's war medal is missing! Burl stole it! Burl stole it!"

"Burl, have you got Freddie's medal?" Father questioned Burl with an impatience new to him.

"No, boss. I don't know nothin' about it."

"Yes, you do." Freddie stood beside Father and me. "I saw Hank give it to him. They dangled it in front of me before they hid it. Mr. Kross, it's purple, shaped like a heart with gold around the edges."

Burl said, "I tell you, boss. I ain't seen the da-dern thing."

"Any of you boys bother Freddie again, and you're finished

here," Father said. "I've put up with enough of this foolishness. There's work to be done." Father walked away, leaving Freddie still shaking beside me.

"Ada, he did take it!" Freddie broke down and cried. I had never seen a boy cry real tears. I watched the tears roll down his cheeks and I wanted justice.

"It was all I had of him." The sweat on Freddie's hands irritated his eyes when he rubbed them. They grew redder and puffy, his glasses magnifying his misery. "What am I going to do without my medal?"

"You don't need the medal to join the foreign legion," I said. "Don't cry. We might find that medal of yours yet."

I found Burl hoeing in the east field and decided to try my charm—whatever that meant. Burl was hardly moving as he leaned against the hoe handle, staring into the dirt. It was insane for me to try to persuade him to do the right thing.

"Burl, I'm here to ask you to give that medal back. It's all Freddie has of his dead daddy."

"Don't come around me, askin' for my sympathy." Burl didn't look up. He dug the hoe blade deep into the hard, black earth.

"I guess I was mistaken about you. I thought you had feelings," I said. "I thought maybe you'd understand since your daddy is dead, too."

Burl's body became rigid. The sun beat like a pulse on us; I could hear the silent strain.

"Don't ever mention my old man again," Burl mumbled. "You understand?"

I backed away and ran to where Mr. Pearl was working.

"We're all losing control of our senses," I said. "I'm trying to be a teenager before I turn thirteen. Freddie wants to be a soldier, which has to be the most unpopular profession in this universe. Beth loves a boy she hasn't met yet. And Mother's having a baby she doesn't need."

"Ada, what brought this rage about?" Mr. Pearl had been working contented as a buttercup until I arrived.

"Burl scared me. Not that there's anything new about that. He and Hank stole Freddie's war medal. All I said to him was that I thought he'd give it back since his own daddy is dead, too. You'd think I'd stuck a dagger into him. I suppose we'll all have to suffer for Burl's unhealed wounds."

Mr. Pearl slowly closed his eyes to me and the light of day. I could sense the same painful rise of all his senses.

"Ada, stay away from Burl. Don't ever talk to him about his daddy again."

"All right," I said. I knew Mr. Pearl's seriousness wasn't to be meddled with. "I didn't mean any harm. I only wanted to help Freddie."

REXY WAS SITTING on a bushel basket outside the front door of the barn, her long bony leg propped up and her chin resting on her knee, when I walked out to feed Puddin. Her pale eyes followed me in to where I found Puddin missing from the premises. I searched through the other crates, hoping that someone had placed Puddin's cage among them by mistake and at the same time feeling furious that someone would actually do such a careless thing. Then Rexy walked in.

"I tried to stop those wild boys, but I ain't got no power over any of them. They don't listen to me." Her angry eyes saddened.

"Rexy, what do you mean?"

"I was goin' to tell your dad when he came in from the field. I hope you won't blame me, Ada."

"Rexy, tell me what you're talking about." I was ready to shake her until the words tumbled out.

"That sneakin' Hank picked up your pigeon, melon crate and all. I heard Burl tell him to do it. Then Burl put it in his car and Burl high-tailed it out of here as fast as he could. Both of 'em ought to be hung by their heels. They're no good, ornery and mean. I'm sorry it had to happen, Ada."

I knew it had been just a matter of time until it happened.

"It's not your fault, Rexy. I've been waiting for Burl to do something rotten. Just promise me you won't tell Dad. I'll tell him in a day or so after I think of a way to get my pigeon back."

"Sure, Ada. I won't breathe a word of it. I hope you can do it," she said as she sullenly walked out to where her ride waited.

I could have run directly to Father. It would have been easy to lay the burden on him. But Burl would only deny taking Puddin; it was Rexy's word against his. And Father would have to choose between justice for a worthless pigeon and the lettuce crop that might go unharvested without the workers he needed. Five thousand tomato plants might smother from the weeds because there wasn't enough help to do the hoeing.

Beth was raking with exuberant strokes around the Stuckeys' grape arbor when I came between two pine trees and rushed to her side, saying I had to talk to someone. She dropped her rake, and together we walked into the pine garden and sat down beside the cement pond.

"What's wrong, Ada? Your hands are shaking." She wrapped her two small hands around mine and tried to stop the chill.

"Burl has my pigeon," I said. "Rexy saw Hank take it cage and all and put it in Burl's car."

"That scalawag! Does he expect you to beg for it?" Beth threw a stone angrily into the tiny pond and shook the sky's reflection. "I'd say go after it, but it's almost impossible to track down someone who lives in a car, even if the car sticks out like a sore thumb." Beth began chewing on her own thumbnail.

"What do you think Burl will do?" I said.

"Burl's most merciful act would be to let Puddin loose. But he's contemptible enough to kill it," Beth said.

"Or he could feed my pigeon to his rat. Surely even Burl wouldn't be mean enough to do that!"

"If we could only find him. But we don't have any transportation of our own." Beth sighed before she looked at me again. "I was hoping to capture a pigeon of my own soon," she said with false enthusiasm. "Why don't we catch two instead?" She saw me scowl unappreciatively. "Oh . . . I know, Ada. It wouldn't be the same."

I shook my head in hopelessness.

"I feel as helpless as you." Beth saw a mist covering my eyes. "But I'll try to think of something."

I HAD NEVER LOST something I loved or had it taken. Puddin was the first. By noon the next day I was inconsolable. I rushed to the pin oaks to talk to Mr. Pearl. He was sipping from his thermos cup, his metal lunch bucket open with fresh sandwiches—always extra for Tippy Ten and me, but even more lately for Beth and Freddie.

"Puddin is gone," I said. The leaves stirred my emotions even more with their sighing sounds. "Hank and Burl took it cage and all."

Mr. Pearl was silent for the longest time. I lay my head against his shoulder and he stroked my hair.

"Puddin is bound to be dead." There was no hope left in me. I was waiting for Mr. Pearl to take the pain away. "I suppose it is better off dead than at Burl's mercy."

"Tell your daddy," Mr. Pearl said optimistically enough to make me angry. "Maybe the bird ain't dead. Maybe Burl took it for meanness but didn't hurt it."

"You're too good-hearted," I said. His strengths seemed to be his weaknesses. "Don't you know that being kind only causes you pain? Good doesn't win in the end." I pulled away from him. "I want to finish this war with Burl Higgins once and for all. I want him to do some suffering."

"Feudin' with Burl ain't goin' to bring the pigeon back," Mr. Pearl said. "Ada, let your daddy handle it."

"No. He's just like you. He's got a big heart but no common sense when it somes to meanness."

"Are we really so bad?" Mr. Pearl tried to laugh off my insults. His eyes tore away my defenses and I buried my face in his chest.

"I miss my little bird," I said. I wiped and rewiped my eyes on his shirt. "I'm sorry for the things I said."

"That's all right. Remember that verse? Fret not thyself because of evildoers."

"I remember." I tried to listen. There was a spell of drowsiness in the breeze. The trees swayed.

"For they shall soon be cut down like the grass, and wither like the green herb. Cease from anger and forsake wrath: fret not thyself in any way to do evil." He put his long arms around me and spoke the words softly, like a lullaby.

"For the Lord loveth justice and forsaketh not his saints; they are preserved forever, but the seed of the wicked shall be cut off."

CHAPTER 13

"I THOUGHT YOU'D NEVER GET HOME." I jumped out from behind my usual spying bush as Beth stepped off the school bus the same afternoon.

"Ada, you scared me! Any news about your pigeon?" She switched the weight of her books from one arm to the other with agitation. "I've thought about it all day. I wish there was something I could do. Personally, I'd like to poke pins in Burl." She was as serious as sin.

"Beth, are you afraid of rats?" I asked in earnest. By that time she was at my side and my feet had fallen in step with hers.

"I don't know. I've only seen pictures of them in the encyclopedia. Why do you ask?"

"Because in a few minutes—with your help—I'm going to kidnap Burl's indecent rat. Are you game?" I tried not to sound as desperate for an accomplice as I felt.

"Ada! This is too serious to be a game. Your whole plan could turn into something shocking if Burl were to catch you in the act." She stopped in her tracks to afford a frown, but it soon turned into a mischevious grin. "But if you must," she paused before committing herself, "we must. What part do I play in this scheme of yours? It sounds risky. Rats bite and they carry rabies. And with rabies you foam at the mouth and have to be quickly put out of your misery."

"First of all, I need to borrow one of your rabbit hutches," I said, feeling a bit revived. "Then I need you to be a lookout. I'll do the dirty work. You're used to taking chances, Beth, and Burl leaves in half an hour."

"So soon!" She hadn't anticipated such immediate action. "All right, Ada. If that's the only way." She set her books and parcels in the fork of a pine tree and we hurried to the outbuilding behind the apple barn, where we chose the smallest rabbit hutch. We then took a shortcut through the pine break and the fields, stepping lightly through the poison ivy.

"Ada, what will this accomplish? That's all I'm asking." Beth's face was redder than a radish. I could sense that she was having second thoughts as we crossed the mushmelon field.

"Burl will have to return my pigeon as ransom for his rat—it's that simple. And if Amos is missing from Burl's car, Burl can't possibly feed my pigeon to it—that is if he hasn't already." We walked faster.

"How is Burl to understand what you're demanding?" Beth asked. I wasn't sure she was capable of withstanding the pressures of crime.

"I've written a ransom note." I patted the back pocket of my shorts with my free hand. "The note says, 'If you want to see your rat alive again, return the pigeon tomorrow.'"

"Aren't you afraid?" Beth asked.

"I'm petrified. But it's a matter of life and death."

The word *death* stuck to the roof of my mouth like stale bread.

"Remember," I said to Beth when we were a stone's throw from the car, "you're the lookout. Burl's working behind the barn, but if he should happen to go to the water well for a drink, he could see every move I'm making."

"What should I do if I see Burl coming?" Beth asked.

"Cough. That won't be too obvious." I moved closer to the car.

"I'm ready when you are." Beth tried to pose nonchalantly against the telephone pole and look toward the field. "The coast is clear." She waved her hand to urge me on.

I opened the door on the driver's seat, and one whiff of Burl's car's breath made me want my asthma mask. The car was filled with fumes of spoiled garbage, beer, and other foul substances—a putrid smell so intense it burned my eyes.

I scooted the rabbit hutch across the seat, close enough to the glove compartment to trap the rat. Then I pushed the button of the glove compartment door. At first it jammed, and I instinctively heard scratching sounds coming from inside which made my nervousness rise. I pushed the glove compartment button again.

"It's coming," I said out loud.

The door flapped open, but before I had positioned the hutch against the opening, a long plump rat hopped out onto the seat and looked up at me with dull black eyes. For the next few moments there was neither sound nor movement on either side of the seat. Finally I said, "Nice rat," in hopes that it was.

"What's going on in there?" Beth yelled from outside. The plan was taking entirely too long.

"Amos is loose in here." I raised my voice enough for her to hear.

At the mention of his name, Amos perked up his head and moved an inch toward me. I sucked in my breath and held it in a frozen panic. I remembered Beth saying that rats carried rabies, but Amos looked perfectly healthy, not bony, undernourished or diseased. He seemed harmless, but then I didn't know how a rabid rat acted.

Beth began to cough and I jumped inside my skin. There wasn't time left. I opened the door and immediately Amos ran toward me, digging his claws into my bare thighs and brushing my arm with the tip of his hairless tail as he leaped out of the car. He landed in the cinders of our drive and headed in the direction of the barn. I could feel a hot nervous rash spread over my skin, and I bit my hand to stop a scream.

Beth's mouth was wide with awe. "My word." She seemed stunned from the sight of it. "Its tail must have been a foot long! The rats in the encyclopedia look like mice with malnutrition compared to that one!"

By that time I had closed the glove compartment door, placed the ransom note on the dash, removed the hutch from the car's interior, and then—cautiously, but with the same haste—shut the sagging door on Burl's car.

"What will Burl do when he finds the note?" Beth stood close by me, watching me work. "You did leave a note, didn't you? Burl won't have any way of knowing we don't have his rat." She took the hutch from my shaking hands and hid it behind a nearby bush.

"It's up to Burl to make the next move. The note is inside." I felt little satisfaction. "Why did you cough? I thought Burl was coming."

"I sincerely had to cough, so I covered my mouth, hoping that you wouldn't hear it. I'm sorry that I messed things up." By that time I was near the point of collapse. Beth took hold of my arm and helped balance my buckling knees. I steadied myself and walked directly to the water faucet, connected the garden hose to the spigot, and handed the hose to Beth.

"Squirt me! Quick! I feel filthy after sitting in that stinking car and being touched by that scroungy rat."

Beth took the hose. In no time, I was soaking wet and cleansed, but not from the memory of it.

BETH AND I HID in the barn loft and listened for the fieldhands to leave at quitting time. Hank left with Burl and if they found the ransom note, they did not tarry. They were gone before the other fieldhands could make tracks.

"I wonder when he'll find the note," Beth said. She and I were lying on our stomachs in the dimness.

"Probably tonight." I put my elbows deeper into the straw and something crackled.

"What's this?" I pulled out a piece of paper with a familiar feel to it. "It's money," I said. I held it up to the beams of light. "Ten dollars!"

"Do you feel any more where that came from?" Beth asked. Our hands searched through the straw without any success.

"I suppose the money could have been up here for years," I thought out loud. "No one comes up here anymore."

"But this ten-dollar bill is crisp and new. Listen to it crunch." Beth was as perplexed as I was.

"I want you to keep this ten dollars, Beth. It will help repay you for the shoes I borrowed for Mother."

"No, Ada. I couldn't. You've already repaid me. Remember?"

"You can and you will. Now take it."

"Well, there is a pair of shoes in Helen Winter's window that I just love. I could put them in layaway with this money, and the other. You know, the last day of Eagle Creek is next Friday. For the sake of Steve Sasser, thank you." I squeezed the money into her hand. She was hungry for it.

"Here comes Freddie and Mr. Pearl," I said. I could hear Freddie trying to sing while Mr. Pearl whistled. Father had assigned Freddie to work at Mr. Pearl's side, and since that change, Freddie seemed to actually enjoy his job. He and Mr. Pearl had become pals.

"Ada, where are you?" Freddie shouted at the top of his lungs. "Mr. Pearl's going to cook our dinner on an open fire tonight, if you want him to." He repeated the news again and again until I came out from cover.

THAT NIGHT Freddie, Beth, and I had dinner with Mr. Pearl. We made a large campfire in the open field, and there were fried potatoes, a vegetable stew of Mr. Pearl's creation, and roasted marshmallows for dessert. It was near the close of our festivity that the talk turned to angels.

"Mr. Pearl, Abe told me you were strange." Freddie was not being unkind. He was eating marshmallows the way most people indulge in after-dinner mints. "But Rexy told me why. She said that you saw an angel."

"Do you think it is so strange to see something supernatural?" Mr. Pearl questioned him with some caution.

"I never thought about it before," Freddie said. "I believe in ghosts, so why not angels?"

"I believe in angels, too," Beth said. She looked at me with revelation. "So that's why there are angels on your book case!"

I nodded.

"They are with us all the time," Mr. Pearl said. "We just don't see 'em."

"But you saw one," Beth said.

"Only once, and only for a minute."

"Was it a blinding light?" Beth asked. She rested her chin in her hands in a listening position.

"What did it look like?" Freddie was the most serious I had ever seen him.

Before Mr. Pearl began, he was silent, almost in meditation. Whenever he told the story of the angel, he drew his breaths deeper, as if the words were buried deep within where they would never fail him.

"It was nearly thirteen years ago, on the sixth of May. I was hoeing in the east field. It was cloudy, and I was expecting rain any minute, when I looked up and saw one strange and bright sunbeam fall from the clouds. I looked again and it was no sunbeam that I saw. It was a strange white light coming toward me."

"How close was it?" Freddie asked with believing eyes.

"Shhhhhhh." Beth leaned toward the flames.

"Close enough that I could have touched it with my hoe," Mr. Pearl said, capturing again the wonder of it for me.

"When the light settled beside me, it became the most beautiful heavenly being, nearly seven feet high, strong build like a warrior with all-knowing, gentle eyes. It seemed to float. The hem of its garment moved in a current like lightning. Somehow I knew not to touch it."

"Did the angel have wings?" Beth asked him.

"It didn't have wings, and it was neither a man or a woman. It was a creation all of its own. It stood before me just as real as we are."

"What did you do then?" Freddie had coaxed Tippy Ten over to him with a marshmallow and he was blindly smoothing the dog's fur, not taking his eyes off Mr. Pearl.

"I got down on my knees and bowed my head to pray. Then I suddenly felt like I was touched by it, like my very life was going in and out of me all at the same time. When the feeling stopped, I looked up and watched the angel leave. The beam of light got smaller until it was only a speck of light. Then there was nothing. Not even a footprint. Just the memory of it."

"Mr. Pearl, d-did the angel speak?" Beth's eyes were moist and reverent.

"No. Not in words. Just feelings," Mr. Pearl said.

I had imagined seeing that angel a thousand times. I knew how soft its gown must feel, probably made of clouds or some kind of heavenly cloth. And how its hands were hands that had touched God; hands holier than the Bible. I sat next to Mr. Pearl, loving him and the story completely. The more of the story he told, the more emptiness I felt within, as if he took from me to give to them. It had been years since Mr. Pearl had shared the story with a stranger. Instead, he has always retold the story to me. Freddie's and Beth's enthusiasm was visible; it radiated from their eyes and skin. But did they truly believe him?

"If it had been anybody but you, I wouldn't have believed it," Freddie said, to my relief.

"It's good you do, son. The more you believe, the more possible things become."

"That means there really is an eternity!" Beth looked up at the countless stars. "But what did the visit of the angel mean?"

"Maybe it means enough just to be allowed to see one." Mr. Pearl smiled. "Everything seemed different once I'd seen it."

"That must mean you're special," Beth said. "You're one of God's chosen."

The wind, the birds, and all the night sounds were hushed. It was so quiet that we all jumped when the fire suddenly popped.

"No. I think everybody's got the same privilege. I'm just an old worn-out fieldhand." He smiled again; his eyes had that homesick look that made me want to cry.

"Of course the story of the angel is supposed to be kept quiet," I said. I felt the need to protect it.

"You're not ashamed of it, are you?" Beth was on the verge of disappointment.

"No!" I reassured her. "But most people don't believe in angels. They think Mr. Pearl is losing his mind. So we only tell special people who will appreciate it."

"We won't tell anyone," Freddie said solemnly. "I wish my guardian angel would come to my rescue when Burl and Hank pounce on me." We were all fantasizing with those possibilities.

"Thou shalt not be afraid for the terror by night; nor for the arrow that flieth by day." I recited a verse from Scripture that Mr. Pearl had committed to memory. "Remember that one, Mr. Pearl?" I asked. I felt secure knowing that there were still hundreds of angel verses that we had in common.

"Ada, that's lovely," Beth said. She was unusually quiet.

Mr. Pearl continued the verse I began, only he was like a preacher speaking from a pulpit.

"He shall give his angels charge over thee. They shall bear thee up in their hands, lest thou dash thy foot against a stone." Mr. Pearl's hands trembled as he raised them and lowered them again. "And the Good Book don't lie, children."

AFTER BETH AND FREDDIE had started for home, I helped Mr. Pearl put out the fire. He whistled as he spread the glowing ashes over the earth.

"They believed it." I was grateful and relieved. "Are you glad that Freddie and Beth know about the angel?"

"I'm glad for you," he said quietly.

"Why me? It's your story."

"Because when I'm gone, Freddie and Beth will help you carry the story. It won't be such a burden. When you remember, you won't remember alone."

CHAPTER 14

THE NEXT DAY I HELD MY BREATH waiting to see Burl's reaction to the kidnapping. Burl came to work as usual and labored in the field with the other fieldhands without a disturbance. I decided to take a chance on a confrontation with him, hoping we could strike a bargain. I walked out to the field and pretended to discuss business with Freddie. Then I saw Mitch.

Mitch, Abe's brother, was working beside Freddie that day. Like many of the poor boys in town, Mitch had once worked for Father until he was old enough to leave and find a better job in the factory. Evidently, he was out of work again.

"Ada, you sure have grown," Mitch said. He was working as little as possible and encouraged my conversation.

"I suppose." I could feel my hair sticking out in all directions and I awkwardly tried to smooth it down.

"I remember Ada when she was only three years old." He turned to Freddie. "She'd follow that old man around and he'd whistle to her."

"Do you remember really?" I was fascinated that I had really known Mr. Pearl that long.

"I see the old guy is still working here. Is he still a little touched?"

"Oh, he's not crazy," Freddie said. "He's OK . . . really."

"Years back, when I was working here, he said he saw an angel. Is he still talkin' like that?"

116

Freddie looked at me with discernment, waiting for my comment. I could feel my spine stiffen and my stomach twist.

"What are you doing here?" I squinted up at Mitch.

"There's a strike at the glass plant. Your dad was short on help, so I said I'd work till things were straightened out at the factory."

"Oh."

"Fact is, the old man killed a man right in that barn." Mitch pointed to the familiar barn on our land.

"I think you've got your men mixed up," I laughed.

"No. There ain't no mistake. That's why he thinks he seen an angel. He lost his senses because of the killing, and he ain't never been the same since. You mean you didn't know that?"

"I know you're a damn liar." I backed away from him and doubled up my fist.

"Here he comes," Mitch said. "Ask him. . . . I'll ask him."

Mr. Pearl walked toward us. He was studying the plant rows to see if any weeds between the pepper plants had been missed. He nodded at Mitch when he passed us. Mitch stopped him and my blood froze. I felt like a traitor just standing in listening distance.

"Pearl, did you or did you not kill Jake Higgins? About ten years ago? Ada is calling me a no-good liar."

Mr. Pearl's face looked strained, as if his eyes suddenly hurt and it would pain his lips to move them the slightest.

"Don't listen to Mitch." I tried to act amused. "He's got you mixed up with somebody else."

Mr. Pearl looked at me and then looked away without a denial. He walked on down the row and left me foolish.

"Mitch, why don't you let the dead rest, and the living." Rexy had stopped hoeing to listen. She leaned forward, her hoe supporting her nimble, pencil-like frame.

"Do you mean the angel man's a killer?" I heard Abe say to Mitch. "He killed somebody?"

Rexy looked in Burl's direction. "Hush, before you start trouble."

"Killer! Killer! Killer!" Abe shouted after Mr. Pearl's wobbling figure. Rexy raised her hand to reprimand Abe.

I could feel the tension in the field thickening like a witch's brew. The distance between Burl and the truth lessened by the minute. Burl stood rigid, his ear cocked.

"I told you." Mitch looked at me with destructive satisfaction. "You better clean up your manners and watch who you call a liar."

"Don't talk to me about manners," I said to Mitch. "Why didn't you stay in the factory where you belong? I still don't believe it."

"Jake Higgins was better off dead." Rexy tried to whisper and console me. "He was a cold-blooded killer. Killed his wife and children. Somehow Burl got saved."

"Does Burl know?" Freddie asked. I was suddenly speechless, my heart one solid pain.

"Burl don't know who done it." Rexy said. "At least he didn't 'til today. Mitch knows Jake Higgins wasn't worth the words he's wasted gossiping about it. Mitch can't never get his facts straight."

"Woman, was you there?" Mitch stopped his picking and turned a shoulder to Rexy.

"I was as good as there," Rexy raised her husky voice. "I was more there than you was. I know enough to tell Ada that Pearl saved a policeman's life. He wasn't no killer, he was a hero. But what would you know about heroes?" She spit on the battleground close to Abe. "Abe, you good-for-nothin'. You don't know right from wrong. You leave that man be. Pearl keeps to hisself and don't hurt nobody."

"Don't preach to me, old woman," Abe mumbled.

"Burl's daddy was a sick man," Rexy said to me. "He didn't know right from wrong, and when he didn't think the world was treatin' him right he'd strike out, hurtin' everybody in his path. Most of the time he'd take his craziness out on strangers in the bars, but one night Higgins went on a shooting spree. He shot a lot of innocent people, includin' Burl's mother and brothers and sisters."

"Then how did he get shot in our barn?" I asked her. I tried to keep my voice low to remind Rexy to do the same. I could feel the tears that fled from my disbelieving eyes. Mr. Pearl had surely considered me more of a child than a friend, or he had thought me too inferior to know the truth about him. "On the way out of town, Higgins stopped and hid in your barn. The police followed him there and surrounded it." Rexy got down on one knee and motioned Freddie and me closer.

"Well, if the police were there, why did Mr. Pearl shoot him?" Freddie asked her.

" 'Cause Pearl tried to talk Burl's daddy out. When one policeman went into the barn after Higgins, he asked Pearl to cover him. Pearl wanted Higgins to give himself up so there'd be no shootin'. Pearl and Higgins both worked for Kelsey. But Pearl saw Higgins' shadow rise up in the moonlight, with a gun pointed right at the policemen's head. He had to make a fast decision. Pearl shot Higgins dead."

Burl turned his ashen face toward us; his black lifeless eyes shone with strange determination. Then he and Hank walked past our gathering in Mr. Pearl's direction, and an uneasy hush followed them. My feet were suddenly rooted to the earth.

"Now there'll be trouble for sure." Rexy ran after Burl like a long, stiff-legged bird. "Burl, you always knowed what your daddy done. It wasn't Pearl's fault." Her face flushed with defeat. "Pearl never lied to you, boy. Don't hurt him. He'll shrivel up and die for sure." Rexy threw up her calloused hands. Burl didn't stop or listen.

I tried to walk, to hurry to find Mr. Pearl. Freddie followed me, trying to console me by repeating again and again, "Don't cry, Ada. Burl won't hurt him. I won't let him."

"Freddie, we must never talk about this again, not even to Mr. Pearl," I said.

Freddie agreed wholeheartedly as he doubled up his fist, preparing for the worst.

We found Burl searching the barn for Mr. Pearl with Hank's assistance. Mr. Pearl's truck was gone. I breathed a sigh of relief, until Tippy Ten passed Burl and got in Burl's way. That was when I heard Burl say, "Move, dog, before I kill you." Burl lifted his filthy boot and kicked Tippy in the ribs, shaking Tippy's balance.

"Stop that! Stop that!" Freddie moved past me. Before he could reach Tippy, Burl had kicked the dog again. Freddie was too angry to be afraid. He got between Burl and the dog and doubled up his pudgy fists.

"Come on, Higgins. You've been wantin' to prove how tough you are. Now's your chance. I might not be an old man or a dog, but I'll do for the likes of you."

"Hippo, this will be a pleasure." Burl spit on the ground, then calmly walked toward Freddie with a crooked grin.

"The name is Freddie." Freddie held his ground.

Burl took a step forward and confidently swung his fist. Freddie ducked and Burl missed. "Good job, Freddie. Wear that weakling out!" I yelled, holding Tippy Ten back by the collar. Hank looked at me and scowled.

Burl reassured Hank with a smile. He moved unhurried and slow with sly, calculating eyes. Freddie kept his eyes stuck on Burl. When Burl swung again, Freddie blocked Burl's punch with one arm and punched Burl in the stomach with the other. Burl lost his breath and doubled over an instant, then straightened. Then he stepped back and panted to refill his lungs.

Burl's skinny legs began to move much faster, darting in and out and around Freddie. He was successful when he swung his fists again. A thin line of fresh blood dribbled out of Freddie's nose, over his mouth, and off his double chin. Freddie wiped some of the blood off on his hand and studied it, and while Freddie was looking down, Burl struck again. This time Freddie's right eye felt the painful jolt of Burl's bony knuckles. Freddie stepped back and moaned. He covered his face with his arm and drew back like a coward.

"You're all right, Freddie. You're stronger than Burl," I yelled. Then Freddie removed his arm from his face, and to everyone's amazement he was smiling.

"You may win this fight, Higgins, but you're going to feel it before we're finished," Freddie said. My mouth dropped open. Mr. Pearl must have been teaching Freddie a lot. Mr. Pearl's words must have strengthened him.

"Well, what you waitin' for, Hippo? So far I ain't felt a damn thing."

Freddie rushed Burl, picking him up by the armpits and flinging him against the barn. It was an impressive sight—Freddie's unsuspected strength.

Burl picked himself up and charged directly toward Freddie like an angered bull. He grabbed Freddie by the neck and attempted to strangle him. I watched Freddie's face change to different shades of red until suddenly he used his excess weight to fall forward on top of Burl. When they hit the dirt, Freddie grabbed Burl by his greasy head of hair and began turning Burl's head from side to side. Finally Burl was forced to let go of Freddie's neck.

"Finish him off, Burl." Hank was on his knees, watching from the fight's level.

"Go, Freddie," I cheered, and held on to Tippy Ten, which by then took all my strength, as he was aching to attack Burl.

Freddie punched Burl once in the jaw and once in the mouth. Both punches looked feeble, but Burl's lip began to bleed.

"Freddie, you're winning. You've got him now." I was in ecstasy.

But Freddie's sudden vigor threatened Hank, who wanted to protect his hero's esteem. He joined in by yanking Freddie's glasses off of him and coupling Freddie's arms behind his back. Burl must have been saving his strength for that moment, for he jumped to his feet and began punching Freddie in the stomach again and again without stopping.

"Two boys against a blind one." I was frantic. "You both should be horsewhipped."

I let loose of Tippy Ten, who ran from Hank to Burl, growling and biting at their feet. "Get them, Tippy. Attack! Attack!" I shouted while I threw dirt clods at Hank's and Burl's backs.

Burl attempted to kick Tippy again, but his aim wasn't as accurate. I quickly rolled up my blouse sleeves and repeated, "I can. I can. I can." Then I flung myself upon Hank's back, clasping my arms around his neck, hoping to cut off his air supply.

"Get off me, you little jackass," he gagged a bit and said weakly. He was fighting Tippy at the same time.

While I kept Hank preoccupied, Freddie was free to finish the fight with Burl. Burl got his third wind and both were on their feet again. Freddie blindly grabbed Burl and tightened his arm around Burl's neck like a pair of pliers. The loss of his glasses made him fight all the more desperately. Burl jabbed Freddie in the ribs with his sharp elbow and Freddie cried out, but he hung on to Burl relentlessly.

Hank was tougher than I thought. Even with Tippy growling at his feet, he managed to throw me off twice with little effort. I fell on my backside skidding in the dust, but I sprang right back with a hand full of dirt and jumped once more on his back, rubbing the loose dirt in his eyes. Hank screamed a fit, cursing at me like I knew the devil, but his distasteful language didn't faze me. I clung to his throat, tightening my clasp like reins into his Adam's apple.

"I hope you choke to death, or go to jail and rot for stealing my pigeon."

Hank flipped me around, twisting my arm behind my back. I thought that either my bone would crack or that my arm would surely pop out of the socket. Just when the pain was thickening to an intolerable degree, I heard Hank cry out. Something had thumped him in the head, and the smell and wetness of cucumber splattered everywhere.

"Take that, you scorpion!" It was Beth, using her schoolbooks as a weapon. She struck Hank again and again without mercy, gritting her teeth as she chastised him.

"Beth, be careful." I was overjoyed to see her.

"I'm fine, Ada." She continued to pound away.

Hank was determined to make me cry for mercy, despite the schoolbook beating he was receiving. But he screamed pitifully when Beth sank her teeth into his shoulder—shirt and all. He had no choice but to let go of me and grab Beth by her flaming head of hair. Then I saw Beth's brilliant eyes burn from the pain until she released her hold on him. Hank must have had enough, for he shouted something disgusting to us all and fled to the field with Tippy at his heels. I called Tippy to my side and held him again as Beth and I watched Burl and Freddie rolling in the dirt. Finally Freddie was on top of the matter. He began to mop the dirt with Burl until he pinned Burl down by the shoulders.

"Promise you'll never touch Mr. Pearl" Freddie said. But Burl only delivered obscenities.

"Promise me you'll bring back my pigeon, or you'll never see your rat alive again." I stood bravely over Burl while Freddie held him. Burl's face was a mild disaster, but his eyes had that undefeated look. The meanness in them was still intense and venomous.

Before any more could be accomplished with threats or promises, we heard a tractor approaching and the four of us scattered. Freddie walked behind the barn to clean up what he could of himself, and Burl left work early, looking like twice a loser.

"BETH CAN YOU BELIEVE what just happened?" I said as we hurried toward the pin oaks to keep out of sight. As we ran, I tried to explain to her what had preceded her grand entrance to the fight, but without speaking of the unsettling gossip.

"I had some unexplainable feeling that I should come here directly from the school bus," Beth said. She was still breathless. "I participated in that fight and I still can't believe it!"

"Right this minute, Freddie is behind the barn spitting blood and suffering," I said, remembering the sight of him. The sickish feeling returned to my stomach. "His face looked like a skinned onion."

"But, Ada, don't you see the beauty of it? Freddie fought!" Beth pounded her fist into her dusty palm. "He won. It was worth it. I'm sure he's never fought another person in his life, and to think that he fought Burl Higgins and won."

"I know. And he fought for Mr. Pearl, Tippy Ten, and me. He was brave. No one could deny that." I was hoping that Freddie was feeling the same. "But what about you, Beth? Look at yourself. Your parents will disown you or send you to reform school if you go home looking like that. Isn't that your Sunday blouse?"

"Yes."

Beth was a despicable mess. Her school clothes were unsalvageably ripped, her nylons full of snags and runners. Her immaculate French braid had lost its dignity, and her radiant complexion was a soiled pink flush. Her tennis shoes were grass stained and gray with dust, not to mention Hank's numerous dirty handprints on the back of her blouse and particularly on the shoulder near the torn lace collar.

"It's nothing to fret about, Ada," Beth said calmly.

Then suddenly, for no apparent reason, Beth abruptly stopped, picked up half a handful of dirt, put it in her mouth, rolled it around with her tongue and spit it out.

"Beth, are you going crazy?" I stopped walking from the wonder of her.

"No, Ada. I'm not losing my senses." She spit a bit more of the dirt out. "I had to get rid of the taste of Hank's shirt and shoulder that were lingering in my mouth." She smiled grittily. "That's better now."

When we were safely inside the pin oaks' protective branches, we lay on our stomachs with our heads intermingled in the lowest limbs and undergrowth. Like shy squirrels, we hid, waiting for Father and Mr. Pearl to return and find evidence of the fight.

"Ada, I hate to mention this," Beth said, kicking back the calves of her legs, "but you are responsible for one bad thing. I do believe I caught poison ivy yesterday when we took the shortcut with the rabbit hutch through the pine break. This itching is becoming unbearable. It's worse than chigger bites." She diligently scratched the red splotches that encircled her ankles.

"I'm sorry about that," I said. "If I hadn't been wearing those awful anklets, I would be suffering, too. I guess they *are* good for something."

"I suppose Mr. Pearl would call this a sinful suffering because I got it doing something devious," Beth said as she examine a leaf that hung close enough to touch the tip of her nose.

"It's pitiful how most of your problems go straight to your feet," I sympathized.

"It is, isn't it? But today was worth all suffering." Beth turned toward me, her eyes reflecting an inner light.

"But let's hope we don't have to fight like that again," I said. Now that the excitement of the fight was wearing off, I was beginning to worry about Mr. Pearl's condition. I had not seen him since the confrontation with Mitch in the field. As he stood in the heart of that discussion, Mr. Pearl's pain had been passed to me by our familiarity, and I was afraid for him. I knew how much he valued every living thing, not to mention a human life.

There was a rustling outside the pin oaks and Tippy Ten pushed himself through the low branches. He lay between us panting from the fatigue of the fight.

"I didn't expect that cucumber to break over Hank's head," Beth gasped between convulsive sounds, rubbing her fingers through Tippy Ten's fur.

"I could ride a wild bronco after riding Hank's back." She made me worry-free whenever she laughed. I laughed with her. "He bucked me off twice."

"What a fight!" Beth summed it up with a sigh.

"Beth, next to Mr. Pearl and Tippy Ten, you are the best friend I've ever had," I said to her. My chin was in my hands, my elbows sinking into the damp earth, pressing the leaves and the grass. We were both looking up at the uncountable arms and leaves that the pin oaks were extending to please and comfort us.

"I never knew what having a friend my own age was like until I met you," I said.

"I never knew what was involved in being a friend until I became your friend, Ada. But I'm not complaining. It's wonderful being myself—knowing that I don't have to wear certain dresses or shoes to keep our friendship alive. I don't have to be anyone but Elizabeth Hathaway Stuckey."

CHAPTER 15

I WAS HOPING THAT Mrs. Moulton's reaction to Freddie's condition after the impact of such a fight would remain a mystery to us all, and I was quite relieved to find that Freddie had called his mother and hitched a ride home with Rexy.

Beth saved her skin by borrowing a change of clothing and asking our parents' permission to stay at my house for dinner and the night, which was agreed upon at both ends.

Father was detained on his delivery and arrived home long after the fieldhands had gone. By the time the four of us were assembled around the table, no one would have guessed that only two hours before, Beth and I had been involved in a knock-down-drag-out fight.

"Ada, you'll have to take Beth to Pigeon Pond," Father said during dinner.

"It's a lovely spot," Mother agreed. "And it's going to be swimming weather soon."

"Pigeon Pond?" Beth asked. "Do pigeons live there?"

"No," I said. I was hoping Beth would not insist on staying on the sore subject of pigeons. "It's a secluded spot in White Horse Woods."

"White Horse Woods? Are there horses running wild there?"

"Once, but the woods are overgrown now. It's a perfect place to explore, and the pond's great for swimming," I said.

"Let's go now." She looked at Father for his approval.

"No. It will be dark in less than an hour," he said. "I only want you girls to go with an adult or in a group."

"I never dreamed there would be such a place. I've always swum at the college pool where Father teaches. I swim like a fish."

"Good," Mother said. "Then you can teach Ada."

"Do you want to learn?" Beth asked me.

"Yes."

"Then I will teach you every stroke. But only under one condition." She smiled slyly. "I'll teach you if you promise to attend Eagle Creek with me the last day of school. You still haven't given me an answer!" She looked at Mother and Father for support. "Don't you think Ada should at least visit Eagle Creek and see how she likes it?"

Father agreed with a nod.

"I think it's a great idea." Mother was pleased with Beth's diplomacy.

"Mrs. Kross, we get all dressed up on the last day of school just for fun, since we're only there long enough to get our report cards." Beth looked at me. "Tell me now. Will you or won't you?"

"I guess." I consented with more dread than anticipation.

It was then that Mrs. Moulton's car drove up and skidded to a stop. Mrs. Moulton bolted into our kitchen, making herself the center of attention.

"I want to know how you could let this happen to Freddie!" Her frail face frowned down at Father with contempt. "Who's running this place of yours—you or a bunch of hoodlums?"

"Calm down, Mrs. Moulton." Father didn't have time or space to stand, she stood so close to the table. He scooted his chair around and looked up at her with innocence. "What are you talking about? What *did* happen to Freddie?"

"The fight! The fight!" she said, wringing her hands.

"I don't know anything about a fight." Father turned toward me. "Was there a fight today, Ada?"

"Yes," I answered with a stone face. I glanced at Beth, who refused to look at me.

"Freddie, get in here and show Mr. Kross what he missed."

Freddie was waiting outside the back porch door. He walked reluctantly into the kitchen with the beginnings of two shiners. His face was extremely skinned and swollen. An "Oh" escaped from Mother's lips.

"Mother, I told you I started the fight." Freddie's words sounded muffled and drawn.

"You couldn't have!" She pushed him aside so that she could pace again. "You're behind this, Ada." She pointed her finger at me. I swallowed my bite of meat whole.

"I started it and I won." Freddie attempted to smile.

"Keep still!" Mrs. Moulton shouted at him. "You're hurt; you're not thinking right." She stopped pacing and pointed her finger at Father. "I ought to sue you. He's lucky he didn't lose his teeth or cut his eyes. I'm taking him to the doctor and sending you the bill!"

"Now, Mrs. Moulton, let's be civilized."

"How can I be?" Mrs. Moulton began to cry. I sensed more fear in her than dismay.

"Please calm down," Mother said and walked over to Mrs. Moulton while Father found room to stand and examine Freddie's wounds.

"Mother, I'm fine." Freddie tried to convince her, but he shouldn't have tried to smile, because Mrs. Moulton cried even harder as a result of it.

"I said, 'keep quiet.' " Her mouth looked disjointed as she tried to talk and cry at the same time. She pushed her large son toward the door with one thin arm. "Go outside and sit in the car. You'll never set foot on this ground again."

"Mr. Kross, please don't fire me," Freddie managed to say above his mother's protesting.

"You're quitting." Mrs. Moulton took Freddie by the arm and shook him. "Do you hear me?" Then, pushing Freddie out the door, she left in the same fury with which she had arrived.

"What happened this afternoon, Ada?" Father sat down again and pushed his plate away.

"Freddie and Burl got into it." I tried to sound like an observer instead of a participant.

"And you didn't bother to tell me?" Father sounded suspicious. He knew I was more likely to say too much than to keep quiet.

"Why didn't you tell me about Jake Higgins?" I asked him. Father looked at Mother and they blinked at each other. "Mitch and Rexy told Freddie and me in the field and Burl overheard. Burl went looking for Mr. Pearl, and Freddie told Burl to fight him instead. You just saw the results. Burl looks worse."

"Pearl made me promise never to tell about the killing. It grieved him just thinking about it. I've tried to keep my word. Sometimes I've been tempted to tell you everything, Ada."

"Abe called Mr. Pearl a killer and that's when Mr. Pearl left. He doesn't know there was a fight. His truck was gone when Burl got to the barn, looking for him."

"Then Mr. Pearl knows that you know about the killing?" Mother asked me.

"Yes. I'm afraid so."

"The most important thing for you to do is find Mr. Pearl tomorrow morning and tell him that you love him," Mother said to me. "He's been old for so long that sometimes we forget that he's aging."

"Do you believe that Mr. Pearl really saw an angel? Or do you think it was all in his head?" I had to know what Father really believed.

Father was quiet for a moment. "I believe that Pearl thinks he saw it, and I've not met a saner man yet."

Father's faith in Mr. Pearl was most comforting. I could forgive him for keeping Mr. Pearl's confidences if he believed in the angel.

BETH WAS EAGER to sleep over, and that night we slept beneath blankets piled high as the air conditioner provided the appropriate atmosphere, like a regulated north wind in winter.

Into the wee hours of the morning Beth and I discussed the events that had taken place and those that were to come. The big party on the last day of school at Eagle Creek was less than a week away. I thought the worst of the storm was over.

But then Saturday morning early, Mother entered my room in an irritable state, announcing that she and Father expected me downstairs that very instant. Then she looked more softly at Beth, whose face was ripening from fear, and asked her to go home immediately.

I hurried downstairs with a drowsy mind, but Father soon remedied my dozing memory.

"Ada, where is your pigeon?" he asked, not too nicely.

"Why, Dad?" I sounded groggy, but inside I was panicking.

"Don't answer my question with a question," he said shortly. "Where is your pigeon?"

"Burl put Hank up to stealing it. I didn't tell you because . . . "

"You've deliberately hidden the truth from me, Ada." Father's voice remained cold in a disappointed tone. "I've told you that silent lies can be as dangerous, if not more deceiving, than spoken lies. I had no idea that you would involve yourself and Beth in a physical fight with Hank and Burl. You're lucky you both weren't hurt."

"Dad, I'm sorry." My lower lip and chin began to quiver. "It happened so fast. Would you want me to be a sissy? If you could have seen the fine way Beth and I . . . I mean the way I fought." I felt the composure of my face folding like an accordian.

"You're not a child any longer, Ada." Father continued with a quiet severity that I had never seen in him. I felt as if he was becoming a stranger before my very eyes. "You're a young lady, and I expect you to behave like one."

"And what young lady belongs with this?" Mother suddenly held up Beth's disgraceful blouse, which we had thought was safely disposed of in the bottom of my wastebasket.

"What do you think Beth's parents would do if they knew you had involved her in such mean business?" Father said. "An apology won't do this time."

"I'm not apologizing for defending what's mine. You're soft on Burl. You'd rather take his part than believe your own daughter."

"This is one time you can't talk your way out, Ada." Father was stern. "You've been wanting to fight Burl for a year."

"That's not so."

"Did you or did you not steal Burl's rat?"

"I did! An eye for an eye and a tooth for a tooth."

"That's not the way you've ben taught," Mother said.

"I'm supposed to stand back and let Burl push me around. Puddin is probably dead from Burl's filthy hands, and you can't understand why I got mad when he turned on Tippy Ten."

"You've talked back enough, Ada." Father stood up and I took a step back. "You're stubborn, and that stubbornness is going to get you in trouble."

"You don't know who I am or what I am, or you'd know I did the right thing."

"I'm not talking about what's right. I'm talking about common sense. You don't fight grown men for any reason. I fired Hank today, and Burl had sense enough not to come to work."

"What about Mitch and Abe? They're the two who started it," I said.

"Abe's picking up his paycheck this afternoon. Mitch too." Looking at Father's tired eyes magnified my misery more.

"You're to stay indoors until Monday, and Beth is not to call or visit. Is that understood? I don't have to tell you how disappointed we are in you."

I nodded, not looking at either of them.

I spent the day moping in my room, feeling like an outcast concerning Father. Although Mother and I had had occasional spats, Father and I had rarely fought. But his eyes had been solemn that morning, as if he had failed me instead of me failing him.

If such bad consequences resulted from fighting for a cause, I wondered why wars were ever fought. I had fought for Mr. Pearl, Freddie, and my animals. It stood to reason that Beth had fought for me and against all the injustice she had seen between Freddie and Burl the previous weeks. And Freddie had fought for us all, plus for respect and dignity, which should more seemingly be bestowed upon a man with grace and peace. The thought of losing Father's trust grieved me.

Father didn't rest until ten o'clock. He worked in the barn until after the sunset, and then he worked in the dark until Mother called him in. It was close to eleven o'clock when I heard footsteps on the stairs. Seconds later he knocked at my door and I told him to come in.

"I want to talk to you, Ada," he said. There was still a thread of coolness between us. He sat down on my bed, wearing the same work clothes he had started the morning with.

"I want to talk to you, too, Dad." I could see by his soft eyes that he had mellowed some since the morning.

I tried to say more, but I felt my throat tightening. I did not want to cry.

"Someday, Dad, you'll trust me again."

"Ada, I trust you. Never said I didn't. A lot has happened the last few weeks." He put his arms around me and consoled my wounded spirit. "I know you were only trying to protect your friends. Burl and Hank weren't worth the trouble they were causing. I got along fine before I hired them; I'll get along fine now." When I looked at Father again, he was the familiar man I had always known. "I saw Mr. Pearl today, and I told him that you still love him," Father said.

"Thank you, Dad."

"Now let me tuck you in so you can get some sleep," he said. He pulled my cover up to my chin, kissed my forehead, and walked to the bedroom door. Then he stopped. "Oh, Ada, I've got some surprising news for you."

"What?" I fluffed my pillow and reached for the light.

"When I talked to Hank today, I asked him about the pigeon. He said something about Burl letting it out of the cage thinking it couldn't fly, but it flew away."

"Hallelujah!" I shouted. I was grateful that Puddin and I had practiced its flight.

"That's not all," Father laughed.

"What do you mean?" I sat up in bed and untangled my sheets. "What happened?"

"I wasn't going to tell you because I know how Hank can lie

while looking a man straight in the eye and I didn't want to get your hopes up. But tonight when I was working in the barn, I'll be darned if your pigeon wasn't sitting on an orange crate, making itself right at home."

I screamed another joyful scream that set Tippy Ten to barking and prompted Mother to shout from downstairs.

"Is everything all right?" she asked.

I was ecstatic, jumping for joy and dancing around the room to Father's laughter.

"I can't believe it! I can't believe such a wonderful thing happened. I knew it was possible, but I didn't dream. . . . I've got to call Beth." I ran for the phone.

"No, Ada. Not yet. Your punishment stands true. But Mr. Pearl will be sure to take care of your bird until Monday."

"Oh yes. Of course, sweet Father of mine." I threw my arms around Father, who lifted me and sat me down in my covers again.

"I love you, Dad," I said as he turned out the light.

"I love you, too, Ada. Nothing you do could ever change that."

CHAPTER 16

By Sunday night I was more than anxious to see Puddin. I was not about to sneak out of the house to the barn without Father's permission after the distance I had created between us on Saturday. Instead, I set my alarm for midnight, reasoning that I wouldn't be disobeying if I slipped out for a short reunion with my pigeon at one minute past twelve—although I had to admit this was a sly move on a small technicality.

The barn had a foreboding face at night and, not taking any chances, I had brought along Tippy Ten and a flashlight. The farther inside the barn's darkness I stepped, the less secure I felt, but I flashed the light in front of me and did not look back. The moonlight creased some of the darkness, but at odd angles that only added more uncertainty to my surroundings. There was a concert of crickets that sounded dramatically close and oversized. I did not waste time.

I stopped where Puddin's melon crate had originally been placed and I called out, "Puddin. Puddin," in a strained shout. There was no response, and I felt sure that the pigeon had abandoned the barn for greener pastures since Saturday night.

"Puddin. Puddin." I snapped my fingers. Then came the pulsating sound of wings rushing toward me. Before I could move or inspect the sound with a flashlight, I felt the pressure of claws pinching the skin of my shoulders through my nightgown and warm soft feather-tips tickling the side of my face.

"Puddin, my precious little bird!" I smoothed its feathers with my finger and it nibbled on my ear. "You came home! You're here!"

Tippy Ten was not interested in joining our reunion. He was investigating with staccato sniffs some strange scent in the dust. Every minute or two he would abruptly stop, look up as if he had come to some conclusion about what he was pursuing, and then begin trailing the scent again.

With my pigeon on my shoulder, I moved in the dark barn confidently, feeling more at ease.

"I'll find you a new melon crate, only this time I'm going to leave the door open so that you can come and go when you're good and ready," I said soothingly as I examined each melon crate with my flashlight, taking special care not to disturb the passenger on my shoulder.

"Now you don't have to be afraid of Burl, because he is gone forever." I said the words out loud for my own reassurance.

"Burl can't ever, ever . . ." There was a slight shift in the floorboard of the loft directly over my head. I did not look up or act startled when I heard it. Then the same board creaked again, and dust and bits of hay fell through a crack and floated to the floor, my flashlight exposing it the way sunlight exposes dust particles by day. I knew I was being watched by someone.

I put Puddin on top of the crate and calmly turned to leave, but I had second thoughts about leaving Puddin alone in the barn without a guardian. So I quickly put him inside the crate he was perched upon and carried bird and container with me. I called Tippy Ten to follow me out, trying to keep my voice natural. It seemed like an hour's walk to the door of the barn. When I could finally see the moonlight on my feet, I ran barefoot across the cinders. I bolted the door behind me, not stopping to think how I would explain Puddin's presence inside the house or the presence of evil inside the barn.

CHAPTER 17

By Monday morning, I was free to come and go as I pleased. But with Freddie's having quit at his mother's insistence and Beth's attending her last week of Eagle Creek, I was prepared for a lonely—and awkward—noon meeting in the pin-oak retreat. What would I say to Mr. Pearl? But to my surprise, Freddie reported to work punctually at eight o'clock without an argument to be heard from Mrs. Moulton. I hurried to the pin oaks at noon to share the news about Puddin's return by carrying Puddin with me, a twine string tied to its leg for security.

"How do you feel, Freddie?" Mr. Pearl opened his metal lunch box and pulled out a sandwich. Tippy left my side to claim his usual crumbs.

"I feel better than I look," Freddie said. He tried to smile. "I feel like my father would be proud of me, even though my mother isn't. I didn't mean to get anyone into trouble over the fight. I suppose you're going to tell me I should have turned the other cheek, but that's hard to do when you've turned it so many times out of being afraid. I tried to do what you taught me." Freddie gingerly rubbed the tender skin around his eyes.

"There's such a thing as self-defense, Freddie." Mr. Pearl rested his back against the tree trunk and took sips from his thermos cup. "But I heard you fought Burl for me. Thank you, son. I'm glad you won the fight, but either way you're still a winner."

"My dad died fighting somebody's war," Freddie said unemotionally. "I never knew him. But we've still got his medals. One's purple, shaped like a heart, and when I was little, I would hold it tight in the palm of my hand, like this," Freddie rolled his fingers into a tight clinch, "until I could feel my own pulse beating, but I'd pretend it was his heart beating inside of it. Funny what a little kid will do." He relaxed his grip again and stared at his empty fist. "Burl stole that medal," Freddie said.

Mr. Pearl listened quietly, his eyes as soft as the clouds. The pin-oak leaves seemed to breathe in harmony with our breathing.

"You deserve a medal yourself, Freddie," I said.

"I think you're quite courageous too, Freddie!" a distant voice said. Tippy's tail brushed the grass as Beth poked herself, legs first, through the branches, much to our surprise.

"Beth, what are you doing here?" I stood up to help her pull the branches away, balancing Puddin on my shoulder at the same time. "Why aren't you in school?"

"Don't touch me! It's this poison ivy." Beth pointed to her spotted face, legs, and arms. If it isn't gone by Friday, I'll just die. I could hardly move, it itched so badly this morning. But when I heard the noon whistle blow, I thought of you all and I shinnied down the holly tree beside my bedroom window. And . . . here I am!" She stretched forth her arms as if they were to be suddenly transformed into wings. "Have I missed anything?"

Up until then, Beth had been absorbed in her own conversation without noticing Puddin. When her large eyes finally rested upon it, her face became almost frightened. "I think I'm going to cry." She sat down slowly without taking her wide, wonder-stricken eyes off of my pigeon. "I'll never be doubtful about anything again!"

"I doubted it more than anyone," I said. Beth held out her arm and pigeon touched it timidly, as if it were stepping into cold water. Finally, it made the exchange and seemed satisfied to pace upon Beth's poison-ivy patches.

With the pigeon settled, Beth turned her attention upon Freddie. "I distinctly understood your mother to say that you were forbidden from this garden's ground."

"We talked it out," Freddie murmured.

"You must have done some pretty fast talking," I said jokingly.

"With these lips?" Freddie pointed to his swollen mouth. His eyes were the only spots that could tolerate the strain of any physical expression. "My mother's happy when I'm happy, and I'm happier now." Freddie tried to smile. "Both of you girls are brave. I never knew girls could fight that way."

"Neither did we." Beth leaned back with laughter.

"That just goes to show you that you don't know what you can do until you get the chance." Mr. Pearl chuckled and threw Tippy Ten a large portion of his sandwich.

"I owe you all a lot. Thanks," Freddie said. "Even Tippy Ten."

"Mr. Pearl," I said. "I think Burl would give his rotten eye-teeth to dispose of me permanently. I think he's hiding in the barn at night. I heard him early this morning when I went into the barn to see Puddin." During the daylight hours my fear of Burl was at a minimum, but I knew that by nightfall I would be full of worry. Life seemed safe and uncomplicated while I was sitting under the pin oaks.

"Ada, what would Burl want with you?" He made me feel foolish.

"Revenge. It's not beneath him."

"I don't believe Burl would be stupid enough to come back here. He knows if your dad saw him, he'd call the sheriff."

"Maybe." I thought about it, and then I remembered the early-morning experience in the barn—how I could sense Burl's eyes like two poisonous spiders moving across my skin.

"I'll check the loft before I go home tonight, Ada," Freddie volunteered. "I can tell if he's been up there, maybe."

"Thank you, Freddie." His new courage would come in handy.

"Be careful you don't fall through," Mr. Pearl warned him.

"I want to go swimming at Pigeon Pond!" Freddie changed the subject. "I heard about Pigeon Pond from Mr. Kross."

"So do I," Beth said. "Let's go Friday evening after my last day at Eagle Creek. We can celebrate the summer!"

"Will you come along too, Mr. Pearl?" I was hoping he wasn't feeling excluded from our plans.

"Nope. I'll be resting about then." He tipped his old hat politely. Then he whistled a tune, but it sounded more like a symphony, lifting our doubts above the trees. The tune itself left us with lithe spirits and loftier dreams. It had such a physical sense that I could feel it rise above the branches and drift out over the fields.

The one o'clock train intruded upon our gathering once again, and while Freddie and Mr. Pearl returned to the field, Beth and I walked toward our respective houses.

"Do you think Steve Sasser could ever like a girl with poison ivy?" Beth said, examining her spots.

"Maybe he will think it's only the bloom in your skin," I teased her.

"Now, you're being funny. I'm serious."

"I was serious too when I said that I'm scared as sheep about Burl coming back. It scares me more by the minute." With that, I stumbled over a foreign object. I looked down to discover the residue of what was once a red shoe. It was covered with dirt, warped from the rain, and faded from the sun.

"Oh no!" I wasn't sure I should show her. "Beth, there is something here you probably should see." I picked up the tormented-looking shoe and held it out to her. She took it and examined it anxiously.

"I've never seen a shoe in such a corroded state," she said. "I recognize it. It's one of my missing shoes."

"I have a feeling there is more where this came from." I had fallen on my knees and was crawling about on the ground around a mulberry tree.

"Who would do this disgusting thing?" Beth's lips began to quiver. "Who, Ada? It's absolutely perverted."

Tippy must have heard our excitement from the field, for he cantered over to where we were searching and began to dig furiously as if it were a sport. When his pointed nose had disappeared into the hole, he lifted out the red shoe's mate, carrying it between his smiling teeth.

"This is a nightmare," Beth said as she took the shoe from

Tippy. Then Beth joined me on the ground and began to dig with her hands. In a short time, we had gathered an unimpressive pile of what had once been Beth's private shoe collection. The shoes were chewed in original shapes and designs: one without toes (Beth bitterly stated it would suffice for a sandal), while the others were either without sides, or heels, or both. Beth praised Tippy's artistic genius with sarcastic pride, especially concerning her most impressive pair, the ones she had previously described as having "princess toes."

Tippy wagged his tail with each mention of his name, but by the time Beth had finished her inventory, he hung his head defensively, his eyes rising and falling with the changes of tone and pitch of her voice. I reminded her of Tippy's chivalry, and finally she forgave him.

"Beth, somehow I'll pay for the shoes Tippy's ruined. I hope you won't hate him for this. He worships you, and he doesn't usually take to strangers."

"Don't worry about it, Ada. I'm not mad at anyone. It serves me right for trying to be something that I'm not." Beth looked at the pile of shoes and burst into tears. For a minute she sobbed soulfully into her dirty palms. "I'm going to give it all up," she said. "I'm not Steve Sasser's type. My feet are too flat, my teeth are too crooked, and my hair is the wrong color. I'm just asking for heartache. He doesn't even know I exist, and I think of him every other minute." She rubbed off her tears leaving dirt streaks until more tears washed the streaks away.

"Beth, stop it! Don't ever say that again. If you quit now, you're not the same Beth Hathaway Stuckey I thought I knew. The Beth Hathaway Stuckey with spirit and courage." She was becoming more and more my hope and had lately held all my laughter. "You haven't even tried to talk to Steve Sasser. You've got to go to school tomorrow and think beautiful because you *are* beautiful, inside and out. Didn't you know?"

"No." She looked up at me and her eyes cleared in an instant. "I feel about as beautiful as those shoes." She sniffed again. A faint little smile formed on her lips before they trembled again. "But I've been thinking a lot about Mr. Pearl's angel, and you know something, Ada? Nothing is really that important after hearing about that angel." She smiled again and the sun shone through. "I feel more valuable because of it."

"I do too."

We filled our arms full of the remnants and proceeded out to the trash barrel, where I started a fire. Beth managed to smile as she threw the last of her shoes into the hungry flames.

"I know a nice barrel in your apple barn that would be more convenient than the pine break," I said.

"Dog-proof?" Her smile widened.

"And don't forget that I'm going to pay you the money for the shoes Tippy Ten has chewed. You'll be back in business in no time."

"Ada, there will always be thousands of shoes in the world, but you are one friend who can never be replaced. Promise me you won't go into the barn after dark for any reason."

"After last night, I wouldn't dream of it."

"And give Puddin his freedom from the twine. That way Burl can't get his hands on it again. Or better yet, let me take Puddin home until this thing with Burl is settled."

"That's a good idea." Before she left, I handed her the melon crate and walked her halfway home, hating to see her disappear into the pines. Some of my courage went with her, along with a portion of my backbone.

Before Freddie left for home that afternoon, he cautiously climbed the loft's ladder to inspect for any sign of Burl.

"See anything?" I asked him. I was standing right below.

"No. Nothing but straw. It looks like some of it's been stirred, but that could be an animal."

"I suppose," I said, but I wasn't satisfied. "Try this experiment for me. I'll stand where I was standing early this morning. You stand where I heard the floorboards creak."

"OK. I'll walk. Tell me when to stop." Freddie began.

"Now stop," I said.

"I can see you," Freddie made his voice mysterious.

"It isn't funny!" The experiment was a frightening success as the floorboards creaked sounds identical to those I had heard that morning.

CHAPTER 18

THAT SAME AFTERNOON, after Freddie left work, Tippy Ten was missing, and I began searching the grounds, imagining the worst. The sun was still high enough to light the barn, and I called for him there and almost everywhere without a sign or answer.

My last stop was the onion shed that was connected to the little greenhouse. It was lifeless, unsightly, and dim with one window that had been broken and since replaced with a thick black plastic that sagged or bulged, depending upon the direction of the wind.

I stepped in, thinking that Tippy might have trapped himself inside. The shed was gloomy and the plastic window was panting like a tired lung taking its last breath. I walked to the farthest corner, looking for Tippy, when I heard the door quietly close and someone push down on the latch. The shed was pitch black, but I could hear the sounds of that same someone scraping the gravel between the soles of his boots and the cement floor. I turned around to find Burl leaning against the wall and, despite the darkness, my eyes were drawn to a ten-inch blade of shining steel that Burl was holding in his hand. He didn't speak. He just skillfully played with the knife without taking his wicked stare off of me.

My stomach fell. I felt it flutter down and bury itself between my feet, but my heart was beating so painfully and loud that I almost hoped Burl would speak to lessen its sound. I couldn't move my body or my mouth. I stood statued, the whites of my eyes widening as I tried to return Burl's stare.

I felt alone, faint, and terrified. Then Burl tightened his face muscles, took one step forward, and adjusted his grip on the handle of the knife. He smiled like Satan himself as he slowly lifted his forearm and aimed.

I tried to swallow my Adam's apple. I tried to pray. I thought of all the verses about angels and I tried to believe. Then Mr. Pearl's truck drove up, imposing on the suspense that Burl was building between us. Burl glanced nervously toward the motor's sound. I could hear Mr. Pearl whistling beside the barn. His tune was not as cheerful, but still melodic and strong. Then his whistling came closer and more distinct. There was the sound of salvation in his footsteps as he advanced closer to the onion shed. For the first time, Burl looked threatened and uneasy.

"If you tell anyone about this, I'll get your mother and dad." He looked toward the door and then hurriedly looked back at me long enough to throw the knife.

Slicing the darkness, it landed beside my cheek, stabbing deeply the onion-shed wall, close enough to my skin that I could feel the cold steel in spite of the sweat and the flush of my face. Then he escaped through the side of the greenhouse, reaching toward me and grabbing his knife as he left.

My senses were numb. I could hardly hear Mr. Pearl pounding as he tried with much effort to pull open the onion shed door, calling out with suspicion, "Who's in there?"

It must have been adrenalin that moved me across the room to lift the latch, and when Mr. Pearl opened the door and stepped inside, I collapsed into his arms, close to hysteria.

"Ada, what happened in here?"

"Nothing," I said. But I clung to him even tighter and shook. He smoothed my hair and patted me. He held me in his protective arms. I could have stayed there forever.

Finally I looked up at him. His face was filled with sincere concern and worry.

"I don't care who you killed," I said. "I love you. Everyone knows you had to do it."

His brow broke into a sweat. His eyes misted. "I'm glad. I love you too." And he choked on a few words that died somewhere in his throat. Finally, he said, "Tell me what happened in here." He pulled out a white cotton handkerchief and pressed it into my palm. "Now you're safe," he said, as I wiped some of the wetness from my face.

"Don't hold nothin' back," he said. But I needed time to think. I could not take Burl's threats lightly.

"I was in the onion shed looking for Tippy Ten." I paused and tried to keep my voice smooth.

"Go on," Mr. Pearl said.

"It was so dark, and then it got even darker . . . " I paused again. I knew I could not tell him the complete truth. "Then the wind slammed the door shut." I swallowed hard.

"And then what happened?" Mr. Pearl asked.

"I was suddenly afraid of dying. That's all. I was afraid of the dark and dying. Then you came to the door and found me."

Mr. Pearl was quiet for some time, and I worried that he sensed there was more to my story. But then he acted relieved.

"Most people are scared of dyin', Ada. I was too, but then the angel came to me and I knew that death is just the beginning of some other beautiful life. I was grievin' over the killin', but when I saw the angel, I knew I was forgiven. Are you forgettin' the angel, child?"

"No. I'll never forget the angel," I said. But I was still worried about Burl.

"If we knowed how beautiful it was on the other side of the sky, we'd probably want to go there right away. I remember a dream I had not too long ago," Mr. Pearl said. "It was so real, this dream. It seemed I was walkin' in this strange country, and you think our pin oaks are beautiful and green—they couldn't compare to the beautiful trees I seen in my dream. I remember I stopped by a stream, and when I cupped my hands to get a drink from the stream I saw the reflection of my hands in the water, and you know something? The wrinkles on my hands were gone." He held up his hands and looked at them. "These old hands of mine were young hands again. Maybe when we pass on, it'll be a place a lot like that, only it won't be a dream. It'll be like going to sleep here and wakin' up there." Mr. Pearl thought for a moment. "I ain't afraid of losin' my wrinkles." He chuckled.

"I wouldn't know you without your wrinkles," I said.

"Sure you would. Right now I'm just an old cocoon, waitin' to become a butterfly."

"I'd rather have the cocoon," I said. I put my arms around him. The touch of his neck was like a worn damp cloth, up to his pleated chin. He had the scent of familiar things—tomato vine, sweet insecticide dust, sweat, and the smell of the earth.

CHAPTER 19

THE NEXT MORNING I was startled out of a sound sleep, as if someone had shouted my name and left the room. I had been dreaming about the onion shed, with Burl throwing his knife again and again, and I was relieved to find myself safely in bed.

Then Tippy Ten began to bark and whine outside, and the clock told me the time was seven o'clock. I thought it was the fieldhands arriving for work that was disturbing him, but when he persisted I pulled myself out of bed to see what could be so upsetting.

From my bedroom window I could see Rexy and Mitch walking toward the field with bushel baskets dangling from their hands. Rexy was pointing toward a passenger train moving slowly in reverse. It stopped, blocking the crossing, which was a rarity. Freight trains would often stop as they added new links to their chains, but seldom would a passenger train stall so far from the station.

On the other side of the tracks, two men were running across Kelsey's field, but the pin oaks blocked the view as to what they were running toward. Then a distant siren became more and more deliberate, until I saw flashing lights of an ambulance and a police car stop at the edge of the field, near the crossing. I grabbed my robe and ran downstairs.

"Something's happened at the railroad crossing!" I shouted as I forced the stubborn latch on the front door. Tippy met me and ran nervously beside me as if he were anticipating something. I

147

crossed the fields and reached the tracks, climbing between two cars and hoping the train wouldn't decide to move just then. I jumped to the other side as Tippy crawled between the wheels and was again at my side.

The first words I heard were those of a conductor defending himself to the policeman. "I blew my whistle, but he didn't stop. We were on him before he knew he'd been hit."

"Hit what?" I asked a group of strangers, who ignored me.

"Looks like the train dragged it about fifty yards and then tossed it over in the middle of the field," the policeman said, taking notes.

I turned toward the field to discover the wreckage rolled into a black metal ball. Beside it was apparently a body, covered with a red blanket. My heart began to hammer as I walked closer.

"Can't go over there." A man stopped me. I was about twenty yards from the casualty. I knew then what I was witnessing, but I needed to hear it put into words before I would believe it.

"Who is it? Who is it?" I shouted to anyone who would listen, and the small crowd that had gathered turned their eyes on me, but then resumed their conversations. Panicking, I grabbed a man's arm. "Who is it?" I forced him to notice me. He looked toward the wreckage and said dispassionately, "It's some old man that worked for the gardener across the track."

I looked at the blanket again. The colors of the sky and field began to blur and blend. I turned in many directions looking for a place to escape, then staggered into someone's arms. They were the arms of my father.

"Ada, come away from here." He held me for a moment, hoping that I would absorb some of his strength. "Your mother is waiting for you on the other side of the tracks." He spoke softly, his eyes dark pools ready to spill. "Be strong for her. She loved Mr. Pearl too."

I wrapped my arm around his waist, and he partly drug my weight. His bulky work shoes rustling in the rye and the swish of his legs moving inside his roomy trousers were the only comforting sounds. I clung to Father until he helped me between the passenger cars with an unsteady hand. Mother was waiting on the other side in the field as he had said. She held out both arms to me, and I would not let my eyes stray from her two outstretched hands for fear that I would accidentally glance to the left, where the pin oaks protruded so indifferent to the ugly scene.

"Mother, it's Mr. Pearl!" She had somehow known, and when I reached her she gave way and wept with me. She held me closely and rocked me without a word as I rested by head upon her swollen stomach.

"Ada, I've got to be strong for the sake of the baby." She placed her hand as close to it as she could, her other arm remaining around me. "And you must be strong too. Isn't that what Mr. Pearl has taught you all along?"

After the ambulance left, Father came back across the field. He made an effort to act normal, despite the strain. He put his arm around Mother and me and led us back to the house with a dazed, preoccupied expression on his face. Within the hour, a wrecker came and carried the remnants of Mr. Pearl's truck away. I looked over at the peaceful field and knew there would be flowers growing over the spots where Mr. Pearl's blood was shed, but I doubted if I would ever see beauty in a flower from Kelsey's field again.

FREDDIE ARRIVED FOR WORK full of questions about the accident, putting Father in the awkward position of breaking the terrible news to him. I don't know what was said, but I watched Freddie run toward the pin oaks in thick slow movements and plunge headfirst into the branches, burying himself from view inside the thick foliage.

Freddie stayed to work that day, mostly working at Father's side. There were a couple of times when we were close enough to speak, but neither he nor I had the heart. We acted like strangers, not wishing to recognize such an unspeakable sadness in each other.

I knew Beth would have to be told, and that I must tell her before she heard from a gossiper. The second she stepped off the school bus, I motioned for her to come over.

"Ada, did you hear about the man who was killed today by the train?" Beth yelled excitedly as she ran across the field. "Our school bus had to go the long way because it couldn't get through the crossing."

"Beth, sit down," I said. We sat down in the hollow of the small hill beside the hollyhocks. It was all I could do to compose my thoughts into words.

Beth looked at me and then looked at me again more closely. "Have you been near another cat?" She saw my swollen, bloodshot eyes. "Did you see any of it? The newsmen were there."

"Beth, that man . . ."

"I thought I heard a crash at breakfast but—"

"It was Mr. Pearl," I shouted through my numbness.

Beth sat very still and closed her eyes. Her hands began to tremble until she braced her palms against her cheeks, pressing her fingertips against her eyelids. Just as her face was beginning to pinken she dropped her head, letting her long hair shield her emotions. A quick sob escaped.

"This is a tragedy," I heard her say to the ground, and then I watched her tears fall without ever seeing her eyes full.

The afternoon sky was white, like a blank page without the wisdom of a star, without a cloud or a color—as if the beauty of it had been torn away, exposing a great emptiness. I had, when I dared, imagined Mr. Pearl's death to be gentle. I would walk to the pin oaks one afternoon and he would appear to be dozing, but instead, a soft wind would have come to pick up his spirit and carry it to heaven. Mr Pearl's death on any other terms seemed unthinkable and, because of this, I only half believed.

Darkness planted its seeds all too soon. There were no stars that night, no moon—only a purple gloominess and the misery of clouds. I left the south window open, and an occasional breeze twisted the sheer curtains and lifted them to life.

I covered my shelves of angels with a sheet. To look at them then with their history and memories would have been too painful.

Father came up briefly and kissed me good night. He was weary from making all of Mr. Pearl's burial arrangements—Mr. Pearl had had no other family than his beloved Sweet Cindy. Were they together at last? I wondered.

Mother remained in my room with me, sitting at the edge of the bed. For a few minutes we listened to the wind without speaking. The silver maples outside my window tossed from the turbulence, and in the distance I could hear the wind forcing itself upon the pin oaks, their rigid limbs shivering. I felt lost in my own home; I wanted to run away. I would never see Mr. Pearl's face on this earth again. And life *after* this earth did not matter to me that night.

"Do you suppose Dad could cut the pin oaks down?" I asked Mother. "Do you suppose?"

"You know you don't want that, Ada. And I'm sure Mr. Pearl wouldn't want that either." Mother looked strangely pale. She chose her words carefully, and doing so seemed to take all her concentration and energy.

"I guess not. I do know that I want those train whistles to stop blowing. I never noticed how many trains passed by this place until today. Can't we leave here for awhile? Can't we go away?'

"Ada, you can't run away," Mother said, taking my hand and holding it. "You could be a thousand miles from our garden and hear a train whistle blow or hear the wind move the branches of a strange tree, and those sounds would take you back to this time again. I've lost people that I love, but only until I faced my sorrow did it begin to heal. So will you, honey."

"I don't know."

"Sooner or later we lose our loved ones. Living is only half of it. Dying is the other."

"Is there a forever?" There was a bitter taste to my words.

"Ada, we must have been somewhere before we were here."

"With God, I suppose." I could not comprehend. "Mr. Pearl said he had a dream about heaven and how he had no wrinkles anymore. He had the skin of a young man."

"That's probably the way heaven is." Mother smiled and somehow was consoled by my words.

"Will Mr. Pearl remember me now that he isn't here anymore? I'm going to miss him."

"I know. So will I." Mother smoothed the covers of my bed and tucked me in. "Death is one of God's mysteries. But Mr. Pearl was a gentle and kind man and he made a little heaven here on this earth. Now he's found all of it."

"The angel doesn't mean a thing without Mr. Pearl. It means nothing to anyone."

"Ada, don't forsake Mr. Pearl now. He has no one to believe for him, if you don't. Hold your head high and be proud. Good night, darling," she said as she turned off the light, leaving me alone with my memories.

During the early morning hours a car drove up our lane and there was movement downstairs. I went down to find the doctor talking to Father before returning to Mother's room again.

"Is she sick? What's wrong with her?" I held on to Father's shirttail and tugged at it until he spoke.

"She's having problems with the baby." Father's expressions were strained. He was white with worry.

"Will she be all right?" I followed him down the hall. "Is it my fault? Is it because of Mr. Pearl?"

"She'll be OK, but I don't know about the baby." He walked on to the kitchen to collect some ice.

"Is the baby dying before it's even had a chance?" I fought back the tears, feeling guilty for not really wanting it.

"Shhhhhh. We don't know yet. Your mother has to lie still and rest. We can't let the least little thing upset her. Will you help me, Ada?"

"It's my fault, isn't it? Because I fought with Burl and am so upset about Mr. Pearl. Isn't it?"

"No." Father was firm. He knelt down and looked into my eyes. "It's just one of those things that happen to women when they are carrying a baby inside of them." Father poured me a glass of milk. "Take this upstairs with you and get some sleep. Say a prayer for your mother and the baby." He kissed me on the forehead.

I walked up the stairs with an aching stomach. I thought about the episode with Burl in the onion shed, and then Mr. Pearl's death, and now Mother and the baby. I was afraid the world would end. I was worried about the future.

CHAPTER 20

MR. PEARL WAS TO BE BURIED at Oak Hill Cemetery the next morning. It started raining hard, but the services were to go on as planned.

"Mother, I'm going now," I said. Mrs. Stuckey greeted me at Mother's door. She was staying with Mother while Father and I attended the funeral.

"She's sleeping," Mrs. Stuckey said softly. "The doctor prescribed something to relax her."

"Could I see her? I'll be quiet as a mouse." I peeked in. Mother's legs were propped up high. Her eyes were closed, giving her a calm appearance. I hated to leave her.

"Why are her legs propped up that way?" I whispered to Mrs. Stuckey.

"It's a safer position for the baby." We walked back out into the hallway.

"Is she suffering?" I asked Mrs. Stuckey.

"No. She isn't supposed to get excited, or the baby might be born early."

"Then she isn't hurting?"

"No, honey," Mrs. Stuckey said.

"Well, would you tell my mother that when she's back on her feet again, I'll help her paint the bassinet?"

"Of course, Ada," Mrs. Stuckey smiled. She had no idea how I worried about the birth of that baby.

"Oh." I was somewhat relieved. "How's Beth?"

"She was a little low this morning. She wanted to go to the funeral, but she had two make-up tests today for the days she missed with her poison ivy. You know the last day of school is tomorrow. Are you still going with her?"

"I guess." I clicked the heels of my shoes together nervously and glanced into the hall mirror. I had worn the solemnest dress I could find. It was a navy-blue dress that made me look thin. It was a good dress to pray in.

Freddie had asked to attend the service with Father and me. He rode with us, dressed in a blue suit that looked a few sizes smaller than he had probably worn in the previous weeks.

"Mother said if my suit gets wet, it will probably shrink." Freddie tried to make polite conversation. "It doesn't matter to me. It'll be a year before I ever wear it again and by that time I'll be even thinner."

THE CEMETERY'S GREENERY was as rich as a woodland along a river-bed. The rain had put a deeper vein of color into every leaf and blade. As we walked to where Mr. Pearl was to be buried, I counted five umbrellas huddled together: Rexy and a few neighbors. A small tent protected the closed coffin, and spread ceremoniously over the lid of it was a large American flag, symbolizing the time Mr. Pearl had fought in the war. The baskets of cut flowers had a saccharine smell compared to the flowers that grew wild in the fields.

The minister conducted the service as if it were medicine. But there was surely no cure for what I thought would be an ever-lasting heaviness. I stood between Father and Freddie, wishing it were the week before and I had the power to stop time in its tracks. Once I looked up as Rexy lifted her umbrella, her tears flowing like tributaries inside the deeper wrinkles of her skin. Freddie was occasionally taking long breaths and sighing as he stared at the ground. A wick of sadness burned from my stomach to my throat. When a sob began to swell, I controlled it. The tears only stung my eyes and fought their way down my cheeks—exhausting tributes to Mr. Pearl that left me unsatisfied.

Finally the rain stopped. There were no longer little pellets bounding off the tent and umbrellas, and the cemetery was quiet except for occasional drops. I saw the minister open his Bible and begin to read words that I had once read to Mr. Pearl and he had later memorized, words that comforted us when no one would believe about the angel.

"If I have told you of earthly things and ye believe not, how shall ye believe if I tell you of heavenly things? And no man hath ascended up to heaven, but he that came down from heaven, even the Son of Man which is in heaven. That whosoever believeth in Him should not perish, but have eternal life."

I remembered the verse from the first time Mr. Pearl admitted to me that he could not read. I was memorizing the verses for Sunday school, and I brought my Bible to the pin oaks so that Mr. Pearl could follow me for accuracy.

"Ada, I won't lie to you, honey. I can't read one letter 'cept the letters of my name."

"Why didn't you tell me?" I was six or seven at the time. "I can teach you."

"I didn't tell you 'cause I'm ashamed."

After reading the verse, the minister closed with a prayer that made everyone shed a tear. Then the American flag was folded in the appropriate manner and presented to Father. The people began their walk back over the hill and my heart felt as broken as it did before. Father took hold of my arm to lead me away, but I asked to stay behind for a moment with Mr. Pearl's remains. I dreaded going home for fear of what might meet me there. That morning the phone had rung, and when I answered it a voice had said, "Ada, I ain't forgettin' you. Remember the knife." From that moment on it had been impossible for me to separate my grief from my fear, and with Mother's condition being what it was, I had no one to turn to.

"Ada, I think I know how Mr. Pearl came to die on that railroad track." Freddie had walked up beside me without my noticing.

"How?" I stood there staring at nothing but wet air.

"Well, yesterday morning Mr. Pearl was coming to work, driving his old truck and, well, just when he was stopping on that railroad track, he saw—he saw his angel again." I looked at Freddie, whose eyes filled with tears. "Only this time, Ada, the angel was coming for him, to take him to heaven, or wherever angels come from." Freddie's head dropped and a large tear fell like a rainspot on his patent-leather shoe. "I'll never forget Mr. Pearl as long as I live." Freddie sniffed and dried his eyes with a white pressed handkerchief that his mother had supplied for the occasion. And I realized I had grown fond of Freddie in spite of his faults.

"Thank you, Freddie," I said. I bent down and wiped his shoe with my hand. "I hope you're right. Do you think Mr. Pearl is really with his angel?" We started walking back to the car.

"Sure. Or maybe he was an angel too."

MRS. STUCKEY had sandwiches ready when we arrived home, but before we ate, I asked Freddie to come with me to the barn.

"Before I say anything, check the barn for Burl," I said. "But be careful; he's dangerous."

"I'm not afraid." Freddie checked the barn, including the loft, before I continued.

"Are you sure you're not afraid of him?"

"No, Ada. Not anymore."

"Then maybe you can help me. There is no one left but you."

"What is it?" he asked.

I proceeded to tell Freddie the whole story, starting when Burl had cornered me in the onion shed with the knife and Mr. Pearl had come just in time. Then I continued on to tell him about Burl's threats on Mother and Father's lives, and then the phone call.

"Why you?" Freddie wanted to know.

"I don't know, but there has always been a rivalry between us."

"What about your father? Wouldn't he be the one to tell?"

"If I told Dad that Burl was out in the barn, what do you think he would do?"

"He'd go out looking for him." Freddie looked at me a bit more wisely. "And Burl might throw the knife, right?"

"I don't know what Burl would do. I only know what he did to me. And all I know is that Mother might be disturbed if she thought we were in any kind of danger. The doctor said if Mother has any kind of shock the baby would die. Mom's sick in bed now, afraid to move. Dad might underestimate Burl's craziness and get himself hurt, or Mother might sense Dad's nervousness. They can read each other's minds."

"What am I going to do if Burl does come back to get you or whatever he's planning?"

"If you see Burl nosing around, you could run over to Stuckey's and call the police on the two-way radio Mr. Stuckey keeps in their apple barn. You could tell the police to keep on their guard. If Burl's trespassing, he's breaking the law."

"What if Tippy Ten barks?"

"I'll keep him upstairs with me. I hate to do it, but I'll put a muzzle on him if I have to."

"I'll help you, Ada." Freddie looked pale and clammy. "I'll give my mother some excuse for being gone and I'll watch your place from dark to sunrise. If I see a sign of Burl, I'll do what you say."

"Don't try to fight Burl. Remember he doesn't fight fair."

"I won't. Your dad has been good to me, and I did throw some heavy logs on Burl's fire when I fought him."

"Be careful," I said. We shook hands.

"Ada, your mother wants to see you," Father said when Freddie and I came back in. Both of us had lost our appetites. "Don't act worried or sad. Smile, even if it hurts." Father smiled at me and I returned it.

"Hi, Mom." I walked in on tiptoes. She was reading a book peacefully. "Mrs. Stuckey made us delicious sandwiches."

"Good. She's a nice person and she's taking good care of me."
The color was back in her cheeks. I stood beside her and kissed
her forehead.

"Are you better?" I tried to straighten her covers.

"I don't know for sure, darling. I hope so. The doctor's coming
tomorrow morning to check—oh!" Her eyes suddenly widened
with pain and her voice weakened. "Ada, please call Mrs. Stuckey
in here." Mother's breaths came short and fast. I wanted to cling
to her.

I called Mrs. Stuckey who came to Mother's side and politely
sent me out of the room. I felt like an outcast and an intruder. I
paced in the hall until Father made me come into the kitchen.
"She's having false labor pains," he told me. Then he turned to
Freddie. "Freddie, if you don't eat your sandwich, you'll never
have the energy to help me, and we've got to work this afternoon,
since it's stopped raining."

"I'll try." Freddie was putting on a good act but he was as tense
as the rest of us.

That evening I watched the sun set in a scarlet splendor. I
thought of Mr. Pearl's being somewhere beyond that beautiful
horizon and I longed to rest in a blissful sleep. I tried to act at ease
around Father, who spent most of the evening at Mother's side.
She seemed to be better.

Finally at the appropriate hour I excused myself and climbed
the stairs, supposedly to sleep, taking Tippy Ten with me. I
watched and waited for any signs of Freddie. With two miles of
country roads that most city men would not dare walk at night
alone, it would not have surprised me that Freddie had suddenly
lost his new brave nature. Tippy snored at my feet and finally,
some time after midnight, I fell on the bed exhausted from grief,
worry, and fear.

"Your mother is sick! Your mother is sick!" There was a whispering in my dreams. "Your mother is sick, Ada." Father was
leaning over me. I was woozy when I tried to lift my head.

"Your mother is sick. I have to take her to the hospital. The
baby is going to arrive early."

"Now?" I asked him. I was on my feet and following him down a dark stairway.

"Yes," he said softly. "Call the Stuckeys and have Mr. Stuckey come after you. I don't want you staying here alone." Father was absentminded with worry.

"Sure, Dad. I'll call him right after you leave."

Father had Mother bundled in a shawl, her suitcase sitting beside her. I hugged her and held back my fears.

"Ada, I'm going to be all right. And so will the baby."

Then Mother's face tensed. She tried to hide her pain, but her expressions were too unnatural to be truthful. Father started the car motor and came for her.

"Call Mr. Stuckey this very minute," Father said as he went out the door.

"I'll call him." I waved and shivered at the night. The car door slammed and the motor became fainter until there was nothing but crickets and branches moving in the trees of heaven on the south side of the house. It was then that I wished Freddie had become a coward again and stayed home. I knew I could not leave him to watch the house and barn alone. I sat by the window and watched for a flashlight or a moving figure in the moonlight, but the creaking floors were all that disturbed the usual sounds of night. Then there were car lights coming up our driveway. I was surprised and afraid when I saw it was the sheriff's car. Two policemen got out and knocked. I was frightened, but I went to the door and spoke through the chain lock.

"What is it?" I asked.

"Is your father at home?"

"No. He just took my mother to the hospital. My neighbor is coming soon to pick me up."

"We'd like to search your barn. Have you heard any strange disturbances tonight?"

"No. My dog usually barks and he hasn't. Why?"

"Are you familiar with Burl Higgins?" the officer asked.

"Yes. He worked for my father. Why?"

"We're looking for him. He's in trouble with the law. Someone said they saw him running in this direction."

"Look plenty, sheriff, and if you see a young boy around the barn or shed, it might be another fieldhand who sometimes sleeps here."

"We'll look out for him."

And then I watched them walk to the barn with their flashlights moving in front of them and the barn lit up enough to reflect their lights on the glass as they searched. I hoped they would find Freddie, if he had arrived, and warn him. All too soon they were finished with their search. They walked back to the house empty-handed.

"We didn't see anyone or anything, but lock up. He's supposed to be drunk and armed."

I was too frightened to swallow. I locked every door and window and went to the phone to call Freddie's house. I had to know if he was on the way to keep watch. If not, that would mean one less person I would have to worry about. I worried that he could even meet up with Burl on the road.

I dialed his number and the phone rang seven times before Mrs. Moulton answered.

"Hello." Mrs. Moulton was sleep-talking.

"Mrs. Moulton, this is Ada Kross. May I please speak to Freddie?"

"Ada, what do you want with Freddie at this hour?"

"It's important that I speak to him. You see, he's become a good friend and . . ."

"Well, all right. Just a minute." She sat the phone down and I heard her footsteps grow fainter and then return.

"Ada, I forgot, Freddie is spending the night with a friend. A boy down the block."

"Oh. . . . Well, thank you, Mrs. Moulton. Good night."

After thirty minutes or so, convinced that Freddie must have arrived, I called Tippy Ten to my side and stepped out into the night. I ran to the barn in bright moonlight, but clouds covered the moon as I stepped inside and I was momentarily blinded. Then there was the pressure of an arm around my neck and something cold pressing against my throat. I lost my balance and fell backward against a strange body which held me up.

"You struggle and I'll slit your throat." There was a slur of words and the strong smell of alcohol. Tippy Ten growled.

"Call your dog off or I'll kill him. You know I will."

"Down, Tippy," I said, stuttering and shaking and wanting to cry.

"Take this rope and tie his legs together," the voice said. I took the rope, and Tippy looked at me curiously but allowed me to render him helpless. When I finished, the dog wiggled in the dirt and whined.

I had not yet looked into the face of Burl but I knew it was him. He tightened his arm around me and dragged me to the back of the barn, then slowly, with the knife at my side, up the ladder of the loft. At one point his arm was so tight around my neck that I could not breathe. Close to suffocating, I counted to twenty-five before the passage of air was permitted. Finally we were up the ladder and into the loft. I turned around as the moon broke through the clouds and saw the glistening blade of the knife and Burl's sinister stare on me.

"Lay down," Burl said. He pushed me and my weak legs obliged. I fell into the straw. He stood over me and then quickly looked at a watch. He walked over to a corner of the loft and fell to his knees, uncovering something. I heard what sounded like the crackling sounds of money.

I was truly alone. No one in the world would know for hours that I was missing. Then I heard a familiar moan from the opposite corner. I could dimly see a large body lying flat against the wall. Freddie! At least he was alive. Burl saw what I had observed, and he may have sensed some hope in me.

"You give me any trouble and I'll kill him," he said.

He picked up the hidden dollar bills and stuffed his pockets until they overflowed with money bags. He looked at his watch again and fell beside me in the straw. He came close to me until I could feel his smelly breath on my neck, hot and then cold again, and my own heart rising and falling in fear. I was afraid for Freddie's sake and mine.

Then came the sound of a distant train whistle. Burl jerked up his head and listened. He pulled himself up and me with him.

"Come on." He grabbed my arm and used his knife to steer me.

I knew that he was going to jump the moving freight train to get out of town. We made it down the ladder and stepped out into the moonlight.

"Move slow." Burl still held me with one arm wrapped around my waist. After a few steps he stopped and held me closer. "Where is he?" He looked around as if he heard something threatening. Then we took a few more cautious steps.

Suddenly Burl stopped abruptly again. "Where is he?" he said. "I'd like to finish him the way he finished my old man." With a start I realized Burl was referring to Mr. Pearl; evidently he did not know the old man was dead. Another sadness rose up in me.

"Mr. Pearl's dead, Burl. He died two days ago," I said.

"You liar," Burl said. "I just heard him." Burl quickened our steps. He broke out into a sweat, his arm dampening the cloth of my blouse. We walked a bit further and he stopped again.

"Hear that?" he said. "Over there?" At first, I heard nothing. But then I heard whistling—a sound so familiar and sweet it brought instant tears to my eyes. The whistling seemed some distance away. When it stopped, we walked again. Burl placed the knife to my throat in angry fear. "Tell me you don't hear it."

"I hear it," I said, amazed.

We walked toward the railroad tracks.

"Move slow," Burl said. One of his long bony arms was wrapped tightly around my waist. The hot steel blade of the knife lay flat against my defenseless throat. I was petrified that Burl might trip on his own feet and put an end to me by accident. He was staggering drunk. We moved in alternating patches of darkness and light, the moon slipping in and out of the clouds that draped it like an unholy shroud. After only a few more steps, Burl stopped short and pulled me closer.

"Hear that? Over there!" He flipped me around like a rag doll. "Over there. It's over there! Now it's far away. No, it's—it's close!"

Burl began trembling as the whistling sounded clearly three feet to the left of us, then to the right. He moved me back and forth until my legs were helpless to stand.

"It's too loud!" he said. He was shaking with fear. "Now it's soft. It's too loud." He dropped his knife and wrapped his sweaty hands around my neck. I heard the whistling again, and it somehow soothed my terror in the same way Mr. Pearl had soothed me in the past.

"I'll kill her if you don't leave me be. Stop the whistling!" Burl shouted hysterically. He dragged me toward the railroad tracks, closer to the pin oaks that seemed to witness my abduction as dispassionately as they had Mr. Pearl's fatal accident.

Then suddenly Burl pushed me and I fell to the ground.

"He wants you!" Burl shouted.

I heard his desperate steps running toward the approaching train as I lay on my back in the field, staring up at the stars. They were beautiful, as untarnished as ever, playing winking games I did not understand. But the whistling I had heard was so real that I half expected to see my dear old friend pull back the sloping pin oak branches and invite me in.

Still in a daze, I got to my feet and ran to the barn to untie Freddie. I found him bound and gagged with tears of fear and then joy running down his cheeks.

"Ada, I thought you would surely be dead by now," Freddie said. "But then I heard someone whistling like Mr. Pearl, and suddenly I knew you'd be OK."

We embraced and then hurried to the house to call the police. From the windows, we watched two squad cars arrive and six policemen with searchlights comb our fields to recover what could be salvaged of the stolen money. Another car of policemen had captured Burl, who was hiding in a boxcar on the train.

Finally, just before four in the morning, I made Freddie a bed in the guestroom and left him with Tippy Ten sleeping at his feet, then went to my own room. Pondering, I lay on my bed and watched the night fade gradually into dawn. Who besides Freddie would ever believe what happened that night?

The phone rang that morning before seven.

"I heard him! I heard him!" Beth was breathless.

"Heard what? Who?"

"I heard Mr. Pearl whistling last night. Oh, Ada, you'll never believe it. But it couldn't have been anybody else; no one else knew his songs. It was nearly two o'clock in the morning, and I was still getting ready for today at Eagle Creek, and then I heard him. It was like he walked around our house whistling and then walked on. I thought it was the radio at first—I was halfway hoping it was—but it wasn't. And I heard him. I heard his beautiful song and I climbed down the holly tree to tell you after he was gone. But your house looked so dark and I was afraid that Tippy Ten would bark and disturb your mother. So I climbed back up and finally fell off to sleep. Do you believe that?"

"Yes, Beth. I believe . . ."

Father came home soon after. His clothes were wrinkled and his eyes sagged from lack of sleep.

"Ada, what are you doing here?" he asked me. "You're supposed to be staying with the Stuckeys. And why is Freddie here?"

"Never mind us. How is Mother?"

Father smiled. "You have a baby sister!" he said. "She's only six months along, but she's doing real fine. The doctor has her in the incubator."

I cried with relief. "How is Mother?"

"She's doing fine, too. But she's exhausted and she has to stay in the hospital. In a few days she'll be as good as new."

I hugged him hard and ran to the phone once more to call Beth with the good news. I would be seeing her in less than an hour, but I just couldn't wait. I was so full of new things I felt like I was going to overflow.

CHAPTER 21

I WORE MY FAVORITE DRESS, a blue gingham, with white polished shoes, and I waited on the step until I heard Beth's back door slam in the distance. Beth emerged from the pine wearing an orange frock with all fair colors of hair, eyes, and skin. She hurried toward me looking radiant and wide awake.

"This is the most remarkable morning!" She sounded ecstatic as I ran to greet her. "It was like a miracle. Look at my shoes!"

"They're lovely. Aren't those the shoes you've been saving for at Helen Winter's shoe store?" I asked.

"No, Ada. That's just it. Yesterday I had just enough money to get the shoes out of layaway and on my lunch hour at school I stopped by Helen Winter's, and her store was closed for inventory. I knew it was hopeless. I'd have a choice between my old stained tennis shoes or those horrible clodhoppers on the last day of school."

"Where did you dig up those shoes, then? Don't tell me Helen Winter opened her shop just for you."

"No, Ada, it was a kinder deed than that. I woke up this morning and I ran to call you about the whistling. And then when I came back to my room to get dressed, there at the foot of my bed was a shoe box containing these." She looked at them admiringly and clicked her heels together. "In the box was a note that read, 'Have a wonderful day. Love, Mom and Dad.' I don't have to tell you I was in a complete daze. And then you called about the baby, and that's wonderful, too. . . ."

I had never seen her happier. "You didn't exaggerate when you described your new dress as being beautiful," I said. "Why, it's even prettier than that." I marveled over it. The frock was gathered at the neck and it hung in graceful folds. I touched the hem of it and ran my fingers over the threaded flower trim on the puffy sleeves.

"Thank you, Ada. I especially love the embroidery trim." Beth rubbed her fingers over it in a sentimental fashion. "You see, my auntie sewed it by hand, and she has arthritis in her knuckles. I know sometimes when she sewed this dress it had to be painful."

"She must be remarkable," I said. The world was full of the remarkable.

"Yes, she is. But, Ada, your dress is adorable too. You'll have all the eyes on you. Oh, I almost forgot my surprise for you." Beth pulled a package out of her satchel. It was a lovely pair of nylon hose with elastic tops to keep them up.

"Beth, you are the miracle." I took the hose and slipped behind the bushes to put them on. They were slinky, like silk, and I felt that my legs were adorned with spun gold. When I stepped out from the bushes I felt as if I had taken a step toward my womanhood.

"Very nice!" Beth appraised the effect of them.

The sound of the bus's horn startled us. We hurried across the field, each with our own anticipations for the day. Breathless, Beth and I made a hectic entrance into the bus. The other children, most of whom were half-asleep, looked up briefly as we settled into a seat toward the middle. Beth's confidence was at such a peak that it was beginning to rub off on me.

"Steve Sasser gets on next." She jabbed me with her elbow and directed my attention toward the window. "But I don't see him standing beside his mailbox!" she said in melodramatic tones. She grabbed my arm for support.

"Maybe he's late," I said. "Don't give up."

The bus hesitated in front of the Sasser residence, but Steve wasn't waiting, nor did he make a mad dash from his house to catch the bus before it moved on. Beth kicked the back of the seat in front of us with thorough disgust and frustration.

"The best I've looked all year, and he doesn't ride the bus! I should have known my luck was running too smoothly. I wanted you to see him!" She pouted all the way to school and I must admit that I shared some of her disappointment.

Eagle Creek was everything I expected it to be—alive with students yelling and moving about the halls. Beth's friends were cordial to me, and very complimentary about my dress. The fuss they made over Beth's frock and matching shoes made Beth smile from ear to ear and laugh with delight.

The girls carried books for signing autographs, and while Beth was busy signing one I noticed a boy staring at her from across the hall.

After the girls had moved down the hall, he walked over to her and said, "Hi, Beth." Her mouth dropped open in surprise and a flush spread over her face, but then she recovered enough to stammer, "Hello," and to introduce him to me as Steve Sasser. I wanted to shout, but instead I smiled inside myself and said, "It's nice to meet you."

He walked her to homeroom and I walked ahead of them, still listening to every word they said, but far enough away for Beth to feel less self-conscious as she conversed with Steve, who talked so effortlessly and smoothly. When he left her at the door of the room, I heard him promise her that he'd see her that very night at my house. We'd all then go to Pigeon Pond together.

After Steve walked away, I tried to get some logical answers about Steve's plans, but Beth was so distracted and light-headed from her first conversation with him that she only spoke in fragments. Finally, as the teacher began to pass out report cards, she turned to say, "Ada, what is another word for miracles? I hate to repeat myself." Her eyes sparkled, "Did you hear it too, or am I having hallucinations?"

"I'm a witness, Beth. You're not imagining a thing!"

Beth received her report card and I don't believe she even bothered to look at it. She stuffed it in her purse and continued talking to her classmates, the dreamy expression still in her eyes.

Before I had seen the school in its entirety, it was time to leave. On the way home, the school bus was filled with pleasant hostility.

The bus driver, who apparently hated his job, had a low resistance to noise and last-day foolishness. His voice could have scratched steel when he threatened the boys who were emptying squirt guns on a shy girl's forehead. On the floor were paper wads, purposely lost report cards, gym clothes, moldy towels, and at least twenty-five dirty black pocket-sized combs to kick around.

To Beth's surprise, Steve Sasser rode the school bus home and sat three seats ahead of us. Beth continually glanced at Steve to see if he would be glancing at her, until finally their eyes did meet, at which time Beth blushed so preposterously that I thought all the blood in her body had gone directly to her head, leaving her heart to beat needlessly.

"Why didn't you smile back at him?" I scolded her. Beth was actually acting indifferent, if not snobbish, to the boy of her dreams.

"I try to smile, but by mouth just freezes," she confided in newfound misery. "What am I going to do?"

"Well, if you aren't going to smile at him, you'd be better off not to look at him at all. Even I know that much. You'll undo all the good you've done." The coloring on Beth's face was slowly turning to a creamy glow. "I'll tell you what I'll do," I said. "I'll be the spy for you. Every time Steve Sasser looks at you, I'll let you know by whispering 'Ding.' That way he won't see you lose your composure again, and you can practice smiling until you're ready to smile at him."

"That's good, Ada. That's good." Beth batted her desperate eyes to avoid the temptation of staring at Steve Sasser again, although I know they felt confined.

"Now talk normally, and I'll do the rest." I instructed her.

"What did you think of Eagle Creek?" Beth asked with a dramatic enthusiasm.

"It was nice, ding, but of course, Beth, today was a very short, ding, school day."

"And did you like the students there?" she quizzed me in ecstasy.

"Yes, ding, I did. They seem so ding ding ding nice." With my successive dings, Beth smiled the most memorable of all her smiles. I was hoping her shyness would soon leave her.

"Beth, I think you should smile back now," I whispered. "After all, he is coming with us tonight to Pigeon Pond. Doesn't he, ding, get off right up the road?"

"Yes, he does, and yes, I know that I should. All right. I will. I'll do it, but my heart feels like it's going to burst. Is it dangerous when it pounds so painfully hard?" Beth's teeth nearly chattered from nervousness.

"Get the ding thing over and ding, you'll feel better. Whenever something seems impossible to me, I repeat, 'I can. I can. I can.' to myself. It always helps. Ding." Beth nodded at the suggestion and her lips repeated the words silently.

When Steve turned around again, Beth's eyes were waiting to greet his. She grinned and he returned it with a shining symmetrical smile that would have rivaled any movie idol's. Then he jovially waved to her as he stepped off the school bus. Beth fell limply back in her seat, flushed in an infatuated bliss.

"I hope I can fall in love as totally as you," I said as I watched her revive. "It must be an indescribably beautiful experience."

The bus stopped before it crossed that deadly railroad track, and when I glanced out of the window, I saw a familiar gleam of metal in the weeds near the road. Without a word to Beth, I ran up to the driver and commanded him to stop. He did so, after we had crossed the tracks, and I ran behind the bus toward the location where I had sighted it. I searched in the weeds until I found myself an arm's length away from the bucket container that had carried Mr. Pearl's midday nourishment for more summers than I cared to remember. It was without scratches or dents or any signs of violence.

Bending down, I extended my arm. But when my fingers squeezed the handle I began to tremble. The wind whispered withering wasted sounds in the grass, reminding me of my new loneliness. I straightened myself, hearing the coffee shift inside the thermos as I lifted it. I held it stiffly at my side so that I would not hear the familiar sounds from inside it again.

Beth was waiting at the edge of my lane, her sensitive eyes more confused and concerned than I had ever seen them. She seemed weakened without the right words to say. I was determined not to ruin her perfect morning, so I began to nonchalantly swing the lunch bucket and to smile cheerily as I hastened toward her, but the coffee sounds from inside the bucket and the clicking of the handle's hinges brought back all the memories of when Mr. Pearl and I had walked side by side together, and so I kept it close to my side but I continued to smile.

"You know, Beth," I tried to sound my most optimistic, "I do believe that Steve Sasser has fallen for you."

Beth arched her eyebrows and inhaled my words with relief and renewed excitement. "I can't believe Steve Sasser not only spoke to me today, but invited himself to Pigeon Pond with us tonight. Now tell me, Ada, what he said again."

"He said that he heard you were a friend of his cousin Freddie and —." I tried to remember it all correctly.

"No, Ada, if I may interrupt you, he said that he heard that I worked with his cousin, Freddie."

"Oh yes, that's how it was. Anyway, he said that he wanted to go swimming—"

"No, Ada, excuse me again, but I'm positive he approached me by saying that he did want to see Pigeon Pond."

"Beth, you have it all memorized and you know it! You silly girl." I laughed in spite of my sadness.

"I know, but I wanted to hear it again. It is like music to my ears." She danced a few steps on her tiptoes and then whirled herself around. "I can't believe this is all happening. First my auntie sends me this hand-sewn frock from the East, and then new shoes from an unexpected source. And now Steve Sasser is friendly to me and we sort of have a date!"

"I'm so happy for you, Beth. I really mean it. Maybe all your dreams will come true." I wanted to touch her in hopes that some of her good fortune was contagious.

"Ada, there is one dream I have that could come true, but it's up to you to make it happen."

"What is that?" I asked. "I'll try." As if I had the power to do something so phenomenal. I felt flattered nonetheless.

"I know how much you'd love to attend Eagle Creek next year, but you hate wearing that asthma mask."

"True. Continue."

"I'll make a deal with you. If you'll attend Eagle Creek as a full-time student this fall, I'll wear my ugliest corrective shoes on the same day you have to wear your asthma mask, and we'll walk conspicuously to classes together."

I had always been a dreamer, wishing all sorts of beautiful things, but I knew that I could not have ever dreamed up a more original and perfect friend than Elizabeth Hathaway Stuckey.

BETH RAN OVER shortly before seven, a bit nervous about spending the coming evening with Steve and feeling self-conscious about being seen in her swimming suit. I was sitting on the back step watching the birds fly across the fields, feeling a bit melancholy.

"What are you going to do with it?" Beth noticed Mr. Pearl's lunch bucket sitting at the side of the step.

"I thought Freddie might want it for a keepsake. I have so many things of Mr. Pearl's. What do you think about that idea?" I looked at it again.

"You can ask him yourself," Beth said. Freddie's car had turned into the driveway. Mrs. Moulton waved and smiled encouragingly as Freddie jumped out of the car. Steve Sasser was not with him.

"Where's Steve?" Beth didn't hesitate to ask.

"He's coming in a few minutes," Freddie said. "He's riding his bicycle."

"Oh." Beth's relief was evident. She began to prance around with nervous energy.

"Freddie, today I found this between the railroad tracks." I held the lunch bucket up. "Would you like to keep it?"

Freddie took the lunch bucket carefully in his hands and examined it before he handed it back to me. "No thanks, Ada. I appreciate the thought, but I have enough medals as it is." Then, almost immediately, Freddie looked up at the elm tree beside the house and clicked his chubby fingers.

"Why don't we open the top of it, tie it to a pin-oak limb, and make a bird feeder out of it. It can be in memory of Mr. Pearl."

"That is an inspiration." Beth clapped her hands.

"If we hurry, we can do it before Steve comes." I said, standing up.

"The angel was lost. Maybe it had strayed from heaven and lost its way," Freddie said. He carried the lunch bucket with pride.

"Or maybe it came down to visit Mr. Pearl and that was its only purpose," Beth added.

"Maybe," I said. "It doesn't matter what the angel was sent for; it matters that it was sent, and that's the most important. The angel did visit Mr. Pearl, and he saw it with his very own eyes."

"And there is no crime in it!" said Beth. "Why is it such a crime to believe what he saw? Or what we heard? Why is it that people think it is harmful?" Beth said.

"Because they are afraid," Freddie continued with the subject he felt most acquainted with. "They don't want to believe there's things they don't understand. But who's to stop us from believing?"

"What about last night? How can Ada explain Burl's letting her go free and dropping all his money?" Beth thought a bit.

"We can believe in silence without shame," I said. "That's what Mr. Pearl and I did."

"But if anyone asks us, we should say what happened. How can they not believe?" Freddie was fresh with a truth spirit.

"They won't want to believe it," I told him. "And that is when you must say to yourself, 'it happened, and whether or not they believe, nothing can change that fact!' "

Under the pin oaks, I wrapped wire around the handle, and Freddie emptied the lunch bucket. It was a job that I would have dreaded doing myself, for the thermos would have to be taken out, and the stale sandwich that Mr. Pearl had wrapped with his own hands for Wednesday's lunch would have to be discarded.

"Please hand me the sandwich, Freddie." Beth held out her hand and Freddie gently placed it into her palm. "I'm going to break the bread into tiny crumbs so that the lunch bucket will function as a bird feeder from this evening on."

It was remarkable how efficient we had become. Soon with our combined efforts, the lunch bucket was hanging on a reachable branch looking much at home.

"I don't think I could have come back here alone," I said to my friends.

"It's good that we came here together," Beth said.

The sun was low and ripening, but its rays were still pointed enough to pierce the interlocking leaves and shine climactically upon the lunch bucket, making it gleam like a golden shrine. The birds were intrigued by the hanging contraption, and they moved closer limb by limb to investigate it.

Freddie thought that we should say a few words to christen the birdfeeder, and because I had known Mr. Pearl the longest, I was elected. There was a lump in my throat, but the words came easily.

"This birdfeeder is dedicated to our Mr. Pearl, a friend to people and all living things. May the birds that eat from it be blessed with beautiful songs to sing in his memory."

In the distance, Tippy's barking reminded us of our immediate plans, and as we walked across the field we could see Steve pedaling profusely up my lane. For a moment, I thought Beth looked ready to turn and run. But once we were close enough to exchange words, she greeted him, conquering her inhibitions.

Pigeon Pond was hidden by the grace of the woods. It was surrounded by heavy brush and thicket, but there was a beaten path the width of a person that led to its modest shore. The pond area reminded me of a circular room with woods on all sides closing like natural walls with the sky for a ceiling. Each time I visited it, I was equally stunned by its undisturbed beauty. It was subdued and calm, and all of the forest animals drank from it.

There was a mammoth-sized tree trunk that had fallen in the center of the pond and served as a place to rest and sunbathe, and there was a long sturdy vine to swing across. The pond was only large enough to accommodate a handful of people comfortably, but that is what made it so special and discriminating.

The water was clean and clear enough that pebbles could be

seen resting on the bottom. It was warmed gradually by the sun, but was never too warm not to be refreshing, because it was fed by an underground spring.

The birds nested around it, and at the tops of the tallest trees were the nests of the quarrelsome crows. They would often circle above, protesting our intrusion upon what they thought they rightfully owned.

We waded in, finding the water too shallow for any serious swimming lessons, but plenty deep enough for splashing and dunking. Beth acted more at ease than I had seen her for hours, and Steve laughed and talked as if we had known him forever and a day.

Before the sky became too dim, we searched the bottom of the pond for Indian arrowheads and odds and ends of lost treasure, while Freddie grabbed hold of the vine for a swing. Steve was watching and he turned to Beth.

"This ought to be good. Look at his fat elephant legs." He snickered and waited for Beth to agree, but Beth withdrew her face with a sour expression.

"Your legs remind me of—of bean poles." She spit out the words and turned a cold shoulder to Steve, as I stared in amazement.

Luckily Steve thought Beth was only joking, and he managed to enjoy her company until it was dusk above the pond and dark between the trees.

The wood was full of night music. The frogs were beginning to shout while the crickets sang familiar sounds. There wasn't an ounce of wind, just calm humid air to breathe. I suggested that we leave and head back for my house, where iced watermelon was waiting.

"How would you feel," Steve said in a sinister whisper, "If suddenly you had two shadows instead of one?" We were walking through the woods toward home.

"Quiet, Steve," I poked him in the back with my finger. "You might scare yourself." He shined his flashlight into my eyes.

"That will be the day." He puffed up. "I don't believe in good or bad supernatural things."

"Then you don't believe in anything," Beth said as she stopped to wrap her dripping hair with a towel. She quickly tied it with a turban.

"You look like a mummy," Steve teased, which eased some of the tension. All of us laughed at that.

The moon rose above the trees a pale gold, like a mild impotent sun, but by the time it had centered itself in the sky it shone silver and cold, surrounded by an endless circle of colors—a rainbow halo.

"Would somebody tell me what kind of moon that is?" Freddie stopped to stare up at it. "No sun, no rain, but a rainbow around it. What does it mean?"

"Let's don't talk about rainbows," I said, walking ahead of them. Mr. Pearl had often talked about the other side of the rainbow and how the rain in life was as important as the sun.

"It isn't the same kind of rainbow you're thinking of, Ada." Beth was moon-gazing too. "How nice it would feel to touch one, but of course it's only a reflection."

"Where'd you learn that?" Freddie asked her.

"I don't know. It's only logical."

"Who's logical?" Steve shook his damp head. "None of you are logical tonight. It is just a moon; a moon is all that it is."

"Everyone is logical nowadays," I complained. The four of us were walking side by side then. The moonlight faded the black light of night into silvers and grays, draining the summer colors from our faces while having a glistening effect on our eyes and teeth. As we walked between the branches, the shadows pressed against our faces.

"It isn't logical to be logical," Beth philosophized. "I don't ever want to be so logical that I can't dream or see real things that other people don't believe in."

By then we were approaching the road, and in the distance we could see my porch light shining and hear Tippy barking. Freddie stumbled every few steps, still bedazzled by the moon's rainbow.

"You're all a little strange," Steve chuckled.

"If you aren't careful, some of it might rub off on you." I said.

"Not a chance," he scoffed.

Back at the house we settled on the back porch step to eat watermelon. Everyone's shyness seemed to have dissolved in Pigeon Pond, for we laughed, talked, and enjoyed each other's company.

We first heard the whistling moving at a walking pace down the rural route road. Its song echoed, hauntingly happy, eerie in its simplicity and perfection.

"Must be some hobo," Steve commented and spit out a watermelon seed. Tippy Ten stood beside Freddie, wagging his tail.

The three of us did not answer. We only listened as the whistling moved closer. Finally I called out.

"Who is it?" I almost expected a familiar voice to answer. But the whistling only turned and moved in our direction without a sight to reason with.

Steve shined his flashlight directly into the moving sound, but no physical proof of a person was exposed.

"What's happening?" Steve stood up, unashamed of his fear. The whistling was coming closer.

"Keep still," Freddie hushed him.

"I think we should go inside or run." Steve looked at each of us for support. "Let's do something."

"We can't run from something we can't see," I said.

"Turn off your flashlight, Steve," Freddie said calmly.

Freddie, Beth, and I exchanged comforting glances. A look of agreement passed between us. It was at that moment the whistling stopped, still at a distance. The silence found us shivering and apprehensive.

Steve stood up and walked to where he had heard it, shining his flashlight as if it were a weapon. "I know it's a trick. It's got to be."

We remained silent, not knowing what would happen next.

"Something is here—close enough to touch me!" Steve ran back to the group. I retraced his steps and once again the whistling began, a few feet from where I was standing, beside the tree of heaven. It then drifted away as mysteriously as it came, with Steve's flashlight following its departure.

I looked at Freddie and Beth's tranquility and once again we shared the memories. Perhaps I would never actually see an angel while I lived on this earth, but Mr. Pearl was as good to me as any angel could ever be. His love and devotion went beyond death's boundaries. And there was a heavenly Father who had sent me two new friends just when I needed them. I knew it was not coincidence. It was part of the cocooning for all of us.

And the story of Mr. Pearl and the angel would never be a burden to me. I would remember, but I would not remember alone.